"Stories like thick dreams, stories rainbowing your thoughts into new patterns the way crystals scatter light, stories like diagrams of promises kept or buried, lost or exploded—Tenea's *Broken Fevers* collection will fuel your inner truthseeker with beauty, strength, and a calm determination to carry on."

— Nisi Shawl, author of *Everfair*

"Tenea Johnson's new collection, *Broken Fevers*, is a wide-ranging selection of stories—science fiction, dark fantasy, horror, folk tales and mythologies, country magic—presented in clear, crisp writing, minus all affectation, and electric with undercurrents of politics, feminism, and social justice. For lovers of the short story, don't miss this powerful voice."

— Jeffrey Ford, author of *A Natural History of Hell*

"This collection of stories is unexpected and imaginative, disturbing and poignant. Each tale is a deftly crafted puzzle piece—a snapshot of life and society, where the present is tethered to the past and the future. An incredible read!"

— L. Penelope, author of *Song of Blood & Stone*

"Tenea D. Johnson is one of the most gifted protest singers of 21st-century speculative fiction. These stories are strong, beautiful music toward a future built by and for the people."

— Andy Duncan, author of *An Agent of Utopia: New and Selected Stories*

"Brutal, lovely and excruciating, Tenea D. Johnson's *Broken Fears* is an amazing journey through your deepest fears, sorrow and beautiful pain. And you will appreciate every moment of it."

— Dr. Chesya Burke, author of *Let's Play White*

"Dazzling, gritty and provocative, this collection delivers big on style and speculative ideas. Kidnappers who recreate a Middle Passage experience for their abductees. Immortals who truck with depressed fairies in Harlem. Rebellions from above and below. Loss, joy and the truly strange collide here. These stories are so richly conceived they bring a fever to our imagination. And, best of all is Tenea D. Johnson's razor-sharp prose."

— Michele Tracy Berger, author of *Reenu-You*

Broken Fevers

Tenea D. Johnson

To you

May all your fevers break,
and open what should be

"Foundling" first published in *Sycorax's Daughters*, Cedar Grove Publishing, 2017.
"Sugar Hill" first published in *Tales in Firelight and Shadow*, Double Dragon Publishing, 2014.
"Only Then Can I Sleep." first published in *Love and Darker Passions*, Double Dragon Publishing, 2012.
"Live Forevers" and "How the Carters Got Their Name" first published in *R/evolution*, counterpoise records, 2011.
"Lopsided World" first published in *Starting Friction*, Mayapple Press, 2008.
"Release in A minor" first published in *Tangle Edition XY*, Blind Eye Books, 2008.
"The Taken" first published in *Whispers in the Night: Dark Dreams III*, Dafina/Kensington, 2007.
"Deep Night" first published in *Necrologue: The Diva Book of the Dead and the Undead*, Diva Books/Millivres Prowler, Ltd., 2003.

Cover art by Nettrice Gaskins

Cover design by Bizhan Khodabandeh and Gerald Mohamed

ISBN: 978-1732638853

Rosarium Publishing
P.O. Box 544
Greenbelt, MD 20768-0544
www.rosariumpublishing.com

Contents

Bare 9

Foundling 12

Lopsided World 31

The Taken 33

Publishable Regrets 47

Sugar Hill 52

How the Carters Got Their Name 67

Deep Night 72

Only Then Can I Sleep 93

Live Forevers 98

Release in A minor 112

Wake 116

The Hell You Say 124

Up Jumped the Devil 130

Bare

Strip clubs aren't my thing. But my girlfriend, Luz, asked me to come on her first night. She wanted me to be there for the performance, her pièce de résistance in exploring exhibitionistic sensuality, as she put it. Luz had tried to get me to come for a private session in the back room of the porn shop where she and several other of my fellow students pulled in a grand a week as lingerie models. I never went. Stories about lotion bottles and boxes of Kleenex kept me away. But tonight was special, she said. And she was my first girlfriend. Smart in all the right places and sexy in all the others—just what I needed after eighteen years of yearning. So I decided to go.

When I got there it felt a bit classier than I expected. Instead of guitar rock, soft jazz flowed over the walnut and brass bar. The walls were textured ochre, and the air was clear; only a solitary tendril of smoke glowed in the amber lighting. And the men: no droves of men wearing big, dumb smiles like I'd imagined. Some of them even looked nervous—especially when they saw me. Whoever said women came to these places had never been to Delights.

Luz must have told the bouncers about me 'cause I didn't have to pay a cover; they just swept me through to the hostess, a thin brunette. She led me to a small table upfront, right next to the splatter glass. Before I could ask, a waitress appeared at my elbow with a glass of white wine and a fresh peach sliced into eighths. For a skin joint the service was surprisingly good.

Emptiness filled the stage. I must have shown up between shows. I flagged the waitress down and asked when Ms. Tique, Luz's alter ego, would perform. I had another twenty minutes to wait, so I pushed the wine away, pulled out my sketchbook and pencil. Too nervous to work, I watched a man clean the stage in long, slow arcs. When he finished, the house lights dimmed.

Luz took the stage.

Goddammit—she was playing my song. I never bought the CD so that every time I heard it it would be a special occasion, and now it blasted through the speakers, funking the joint up and searing into my memory as something now forever grotesque. I wanted to close my eyes and just listen, let it be that shiny penny on the sidewalk, but I couldn't. So it became the soundtrack to this:

Luz in her black leather bodice, wide hips swaying to the wah wah, loosely-closed fists popping open when the high hat hits, her whole body dedicated to the rhythm of "Tell Me Something Good." She seems longer than her six feet as she unrolls her limbs, snakes her hands high into the air. She brings her arms down before the chorus, grabs the bodice, and rips it open just as Chaka does the same with the song.

And Luz is topless, and I hate everyone else in this room.

I jerk my head around to catch them leering at her. But they're not; they look bored. The man at the table next to mine lazily swirls his drink with a straw and only intermittently brings his attention to the stage. Others lean closer to the splatter glass, elbows propped on their tables, but even they are waiting for something more. I turn back to the stage.

Then Luz starts stripping, and the men come alive. The skin on her forearms goes first. She peels it like overripe fruit, blood and gunk dripping onto the floor. Hooting and catcalls drown out the song. I'm locked into her eyes, looking for signs of pain. Her lip trembles, but that's all. She rakes her thumbs across her collarbone, and a line of blood beads out, starts to stream down her breasts. That's when I think I'm gonna be sick, but I grip the table and hold on. She's staring at me just as hard as I'm looking at her, and I think if I lose it, she will and it'll just be gore. Not this special thing she's been pumping her body full of chemicals for—not a pièce de résistance at all. So I hold onto the table and look her in the eye. That's when she smiles and starts walking toward me, pulling the skin of her right hand off like a glove. She stops just before the splatter glass, leaving a trail behind her. Another woman comes up from behind and brings a razor to Luz's back, carving off the first layer. I can't see it happen, but I see the other woman lay strips of Luz across her forearm as she works.

And in that five minutes it takes my song to play in a place I never wanted to go, Luz is laid absolutely bare: the fat of her breasts glistening, her veins pulsing, her muscles seeping. Everything moving out from her heart. And it is beautiful.

She keeps her face, and partly I think she does this for me.

Foundling

By noon Petal had plucked fourteen people from the earthquake debris. Even if the other techs in HRO's small mobile unit nodded appreciatively, she could hardly believe the slow pace of the rescue teleportations. In the last year alone, she'd evacced an entire Sri Lankan apartment building's residents within 25 minutes of a tsunami alarm and rescued a California firefighter squad from a forest fire seconds before it flamed into an inferno. Other teleport techs worked to match Petal's speed and accuracy; she worked to beat it. But not all trips through the black were about speed.

The fourteen had tired her. She shifted to release the dreadlocks pinned between her back and the chair and stretched her hip from where she sat. Per protocol, she had to clear the chipped before she could extract any unchipped people. The race always sapped her energy. Regardless, she sat alert at her terminal rig, staring at the quintet of monitors, gaze darting between the chip signal map up top and the vectimeter readouts below. Her hands sat loose on the controls, splayed wide, with her pointer finger poised over the Enact button, timing the millisecond the extract arcs would align.

Earthquake rescues were a special challenge, a complicated game of knowing which person to move and when—move the wrong one and other pockets of space might collapse and kill anyone now vulnerable in the configuration of air and pressure that destroyed buildings became. An Indonesian high rise was Boolean calculus that only a Petal Scott could reliably solve. The other techs worked to extract survivors in open fields or atop intact buildings. Their numbers lagged behind hers. Some had clocked out from fatigue after a single extraction; a few gathered discreetly behind her, watching from a distance. Petal paid them no mind.

As the arcs intersected on a trajectory that would hold, she struck the Enact button. In an instant the man she'd spent the last 32 minutes working on disappeared from the rank and dusty hole he'd lain in overnight and materialized at a medevac unit a few miles away. Adi Taher, father of two, vitals still strong, would most likely survive. Petal closed her eyes and stretched her wrists. At 39, they needed more stretching these days. She took two deep gulps from the water bottle on the floor and consulted the map for the next one.

Not a single light blinked on the chip signal map. Had she finally cleared all of the chipped from the queue? Being a high rise in one of Jakarta's wealthiest districts, most of the inhabitants could afford to be chipped. The quake had struck in the middle of a weekday, so hopefully only a small portion of the residents were home at the time. She'd waited on Taher's extraction to give the others a better chance of survival. His position had been tricky, liable to set off little landslides below him. So far the gambit had worked, but now came the true challenge.

Petal looked again at the building's schematics on the bottom left monitor—both the blueprint of what it had been as one piece and the rendering overlay of it in pieces. She pinpointed each sizable void to perform a remote manual bio scan. Though most of the residents had been chipped, just as likely those people had housekeepers and maintenance workers that could never afford the expense.

HRO existed for them. Though Humanitarian Rescue Organization's mandate stated that they would rescue any and all people they could in a natural disaster, their real mission, as far as Petal was concerned, was to save those no one else thought worth the trouble—the ones who could never pay for expensive trips through the black. For them she'd decided to work with a non-governmental organization instead of the lucrative commercial market.

She wouldn't have had it any other way—even today.

Near the top of the rubble, Petal found a number of cooling bodies, a small legion of cats, and below that, three sizable rodents huddled together in the ruins of a restaurant that had once dominated the 15th floor. Sweat beaded on Petal's forehead. She wiped it and dried her hands on her pants. Slowly she scanned the rest of the building, cubic meter by cubic meter, consulting the locale grid she'd imposed on the overlay. At one of the last grid locations, she got a larger, faint reading: no doubt, human. This person lay in the middle of the building, at the bottom, on the cusp of being crushed and being free. The location couldn't be much worse. It denoted a bleak, new level of complexity. Petal had to know the extractee's particulars to have any chance at a successful teleport. She grabbed her headset, toggled the talk function, and dialed up the mobile hospital's HRO rep.

"Intake," a female voice said, her accent relaxing the word.

"Have you finished cross-referencing the records of residence and accounted-for list?" Petal asked.

"Yes, I'll forward it now. Your access number?"

"2478," Petal said.

"Sent," the operator replied.

"Thanks," Petal said, disconnecting.

An icon blinked on the center screen. She ran the parameter search and waited a few seconds for the soft ding of completion in her ear.

Petal exhaled and motioned the ID reveal command. She'd learned not to look at the extractee's particulars before absolutely necessary; she'd watched a colleague in Rio reduced to tears when a sibling showed up on the screen.

The tech couldn't have been more grateful when Petal evacced his sister, but Petal had been just as grateful for the lesson. She had no surviving family, only a long-ago-lost locket of their faces before the fire. She had a heart, though. Sometimes what you didn't know could help someone else.

Petal heard the other techs react and took her time looking at the screen: a baby, a toddler really, no more than four years old. Due to the extractee's age, a photo hadn't been added yet. The screen showed only a DOB with a blank space after the dash—unaccounted-for life, a maid's child, or perhaps a maid-in-training herself. The record didn't include any weight or height measurements from this year, no body scan, just the record of residence.

Petal called in a drone to help her. She wanted eyes on the child. She'd need to see the pocket that held the girl and her position in it, but mostly Petal didn't want her to be alone in the dark any longer. Petal glanced at the top monitors as the drone left the hangar. While she calibrated the vectimeter to her estimates of a South East Asian three-and-a-half-year-old's median weight and height, the drone reached altitude and quickly covered the distance to downtown Jakarta.

Petal watched its progress as the piles of rubble grew larger and the drone cruised down to the one that held the girl. The monitor darkened as the drone reached the closest opening and extended its pinpoint camera into the space. A finger wouldn't have fit into it, but the camera did. A faint outline of concrete and twisted steel glowed into existence on the screen. It slowly brightened, and the girl's face appeared on the top center monitor.

A shallow gash bled down her cheek, but other than that, she looked intact. Her legs and arms were free, her head at a natural-enough angle, but Petal couldn't see any space for her to wiggle, much less take a deep breath. Her lips had turned a strange hue, signaling the need to get her out now. Petal flicked the microphone away from her mouth and activated brown noise inside her headset. Leaning forward, the world shrunk down to five monitors and the controls in her hands.

On the top right monitor, the girl's infrared face glowed. Below it the vectimeter adjusted and dead center scrolled the NAV screen's crowded array of numbers, colors, and all the custom apps and algorithms that Petal had loaded for easy execution. She'd have to go fully manual. For this she'd rather trust her own algorithms. Mass manufacturers hadn't figured out how to code functional finesse. Her algorithms bested them when it came to complex teleport metrics and executions. Though the algorithms only awaited an execution command, first Petal had to see the right combination of variables, the sweet spot in all the data flooding into her system. She tweaked and waited. As each second crept by, with each breath, she felt sure the rubble would shift and crush any hope of completing this rescue. She carefully guided the extract arc into a better position with her left hand. Petal glanced up at the vectimeter; she needed to adjust no more than 1 degree 3 and—there, the curve of a pocket in time. Petal's finger hovered above the Enact button, its code scrawling quickly by. NAV almost lined up. It would in 87 milliseconds, 47 milliseconds, the arc careened, snapped back before Petal could react, 17 ...

The girl disappeared from the screen.

Petal blinked, jerked her head up to check the drone connection. In that millisecond tons of concrete and steel shifted, filling the void. The screen turned black as the camera went offline. Petal gasped. She scanned for bio signals—nothing. Not a cooling temp, or phantom trace. The toddler had simply ceased to be there, but Petal hadn't evacced her. She couldn't identify the feeling filling her chest, just as she couldn't make sense of where in all the worlds and wormholes the girl had gone.

Thirty hectic minutes later she had no explanation—not one for herself or the site director whose office she now stood in, exhausted and frustrated. She felt on the verge of tears but kept her face expressionless; she'd spent years perfecting the wall between her and the world of nerves and overwhelming circumstances. Petal could barely focus on his words and hadn't heard the name of the man he introduced her to. It seemed a strange time for introductions, for conversations, for anything but finding the little girl. The director repeated himself.

"Ms. Scott, this is Brian Dunphries from headquarters," the director said, moving hair out of his eyes as he spoke.

Petal didn't question why headquarters had sent a monitor for her, but a part of her filed away the information, the same part that filed all the work slights and microaggressions she chose not to deal with in the moment.

She knew she should respond to the introduction, but the usual words rang hollow—it was not good to meet him. Petal settled on "Hello" and waited for the director to continue.

"I'd planned on introducing you this morning but didn't want to interrupt your progress on the Crissal Building."

Crissal Building. This, at least, she could connect to. Her eyes shifted to the director and the tall blond man at his side.

"What the hell happened?" the director asked.

"Lost souls are a reality of our business," the HQ rep interjected.

"Supposedly not for Ms. Scott here," the director replied. "We were told she'd never had an incident."

"I haven't—hadn't," Petal said. Other techs accepted lost souls as an inevitable facet of their work; no one even looked for them after the loss. The possibility of losing someone simply because of the complexity of the task didn't square. She created her own algorithms, went manual, and trained three times longer than certification required to negate the inevitability of lost souls. Yet now here she stood, living a moment she'd worked to avoid.

"I have no excuse," she said. She wouldn't start inventing them now.

"You'll be put on leave while we investigate," the director responded.

"Completely routine, Ms. Scott," the rep said.

"Of course," she replied, turning to leave. As the door closed behind her, she heard the director's final words.

"When I met her I told them no way she matched her numbers. Not her fault, really. She's overcome a lot of inherent limitations, but I can't say that I'm surprised."

That night, alone in the small home she rented, the girl's face waited behind Petal's closed eye lids. So Petal had left the bed behind. Instead, she paced and pored over the episode, worrying the floorboards in the narrow corridor between her terminal rig and monitor array. She could hear the steady hum of her generator, and not much else beyond her own thoughts.

Petal had never fancied herself arrogant, but she simply couldn't believe she'd lost the girl. She had no problem accepting her mistakes when she made them, but her head, as well as heart, rejected that conclusion. Her finger hadn't jumped. She'd had 17 milliseconds left, and in that thin sliver of time, something had happened.

A headache collected at her temples, and Petal stopped pacing. She grabbed an apple from the countertop and dropped down at her rig.

She backed up everything, live-fed it to the server stateside that held her entire teleport history. Her father had been a boxing fan and gave her one piece of advice: leave nothing up to the judges. They could conduct their own investigation, but so would she. Devouring the apple in five big bites, she logged onto her archives and pulled up the day's work. Scrolling past the other extractees, she quickly found her place and pored over the time log, reviewing each reading and corresponding action on her part.

It didn't take long to find the hole in the whole. The

anomaly started at 19 milliseconds-until-engage and ended at 17 'til. In those two milliseconds, the arc had deviated—stretched into a parabola that did not correspond to her algorithms or HRO's apps, moved in a way not under her control. The girl had disappeared into that gap.

Petal could find no further record of her existence. As an unchipped, no teleport tech could. Had she spliced with the rubble around her, fallen into an alternate wormhole, evaporated with the cataclysmic intensity of Luther's Arc? Petal did not know. The tears that had threatened all day fell freely now, soaking her shirt, the skin beneath, and further still.

HRO called her back stateside within the week. Despite recent events her record of reliability and success remained unmatched. They could use her in Seattle, where floods were regular and the occasional tsunami surfaced. HQ wrote the incident off as her fall to mortality. She could hear it in the site director's voice, a tiny celebration that now she walked amongst them, no longer ahead. Her apparent failure had improved his day. Hearing it, Petal briefly contemplated finally joining the private sector and its much better paid assignments. But she knew it would never take. There was still good work to do; so she flew back home. She could have expensed a trip through the black. Such trips were built into HRO's operating budget—but she savored the considerable time it took to move from one side of the world to the other.

Brian Dunphries ran the Seattle office. Petal spied him through the glass door as she entered the branch. She didn't welcome the coincidence. No fresh start here, but perhaps that's what HQ had in mind. She'd never needed a minder and didn't now. Still she greeted him with a small smile and an outstretched hand. He had tried to be kind in Jakarta. She could only prove herself all over again though she had never truly stopped, a hazard of her extraction.

"Ms. Scott," Dunphries said. "It's good to see you again. Let me show you to our teleport unit."

All the interior walls were glass. Standing from the front entrance, one could see to the very back of the building. Petal followed Dunphries farther into the translucent maze.

"We run a controlled lab—no custom work and no outside software," he said.

Her algorithms. They wanted her to press buttons and take responsibility for anything that went wrong. Great. Is this supposed to be some sort of probation? Petal wondered. She didn't know any colleagues who worked in a locked-down lab, though some may have welcomed the ease.

"Is that on a probationary basis?" she asked.

"It's our standard protocol," he answered. "And I'll be acting as your supervisor. Because of your advanced experience it seemed the best fit. I'm sure you can appreciate that when things don't go as planned, there's a propensity to blame the operator. Here that's no longer an issue. Our techs execute the protocol, and any errors can be easily traced and recorded."

Recorded, not resolved, Petal thought.

"I see," she said.

They rounded a corner and entered the unit through another set of glass doors.

The room dwarfed any she'd worked in the last three years, the ones she'd spent in Southeast Asia and Sudan. Just as she'd suspected, the techs looked green as hell. They sat in three rows of three, talking across their terminals at one another. A couple of them stopped comming on their watches long enough to turn around and acknowledge her and Dunphries. Three of them looked as if they might still be in secondary school, and the balance as eager and unskilled as the kids who stopped her on the street to see if she'd sign a petition to legalize metamethamine.

"Your colleagues," Dunphries said. "I'll leave you some time to get acquainted." He pointed to a yellow door in the corner.

"You can leave your things at the open terminal. There's an orientation program already cued; just log on. You'll find vending mechs in the break room there."

Petal wasted no time on introductions. As soon as Dunphries left, she waved a hello to the room, sat down at the terminal, logged in, and tried to take a look at the queue. She couldn't access it without completing orientation.

Petal exhaled.

"You'll find a lot is locked down here."

She turned to find one of the young techs standing behind her. He had a stocky build and sported a plaid shirt and unkempt beard.

"Petal Scott, right? I remember hearing about you," he said.

Bad news apparently traveled fast.

"Ten years and only one lost soul. Impressive."

Petal's eye twitched when he said "one lost soul." She could feel the furrow of her brow and struggled to say thanks though she didn't feel it.

This is what they would say now. Even if it never happened again, but worse than that, she would always have the girl's face in the dark, a locket she couldn't lose.

"I'm Jeff Taylor."

She shook his hand, waited for something more.

"Well, I'll let you get back to it," he said.

The orientation program took much longer than necessary. By the time she'd finished, the waiting queue icon had disappeared from her terminal and afternoon had cleared the room. Everyone else talked in the break room or had stepped outside. Now that she had access, Petal searched across the desktop to perform a proper orientation.

Their archive system was a mess. To make matters worse, this office used Diverse Triage for their queue, a program better suited to shipments than teleport tech. Petal frowned and started her review of the server. If she couldn't use her own algorithms, she'd have to learn this system front to back to see how far she could bend it before it broke. Mass-produced software had broad, deep limitations so better to find them now when no one's life hung in the balance.

Server capacity was lean, and they seemed to have the techs' systems tethered in a way that bordered on the obtuse. She shook her head and stretched her neck. From the corner of her eye, she spied the vectimeter back-up files and credentials. She opened the properties. Last calibration: four months ago?

"What the hell?" Petal whispered. She calibrated daily; industry standard dictated 48 hours. Four months was a fucking crime.

"Or at least it should be," she finished out loud.

Anxious now, she continued to hunt around her terminal, opening files and mentally tracking what she found. The queue stayed empty, giving Petal time to explore this troubling new terrain.

The anomaly showed up on her third day in the office. She'd just successfully extracted a man from the roof of his truck in Oregonian flood waters. The intake rep expected him to spend the night at home. For the first time in weeks, Petal's tension unwound a single centimeter; she took a cleansing breath. Someone had cranked the AC up, and she bent over to get a sweater out of her bag. As she righted herself, Dunphries' face popped up on the instant messenger in the corner of her screen.

"Well done," the screen read.

Petal tried to think of a non-condescending interpretation—failed miserably. The message required a perfunctory response, her least favorite kind. She typed her nonexistent thanks and motioned the window to close.

An ID window maximized on the monitor. She must have right toggled when she meant to left. Dunphries' org chart appeared under his name with a tiny asterisk linked to a series of usernames. Odd that he would have so many, but perhaps each piece of software required one. She shook her head; they didn't even have password chains. Good luck to the person who forgot one of them or to someone trying to track overall usage. With the empty queue she could at least fix this problem for them. Conventional best practice required it, and she had more downtime than she could handle.

Petal delved back into the files and then into the code behind the system. A simple administrative reroute should do the trick. She backtracked through the registry to find a way to track users though their devices, IPs, and usernames.

In an hour she found a worm. It hid amongst the benign operational systems, tucked away from the temporary files but always running with them. With it came malware that would have made a mid-grade hacker proud. Dunphries had introduced it. At first she thought the program must have been surveillance, recording keystrokes and the like for security's sake, but the more she searched, the less she thought it had anything to do with official HRO business.

As a creator of dozens of algorithms, execute programs, and apps herself, Petal could understand wanting to customize the boilerplate software this office used, but she had a feeling she didn't yet care to name. Uneasily, she looked to her left and right, sure now that she was being watched or at least her work recorded. She would have to go stealth. She felt for a mem stick in her bag. Petal loaded it into the terminal and waited. She had to find the right moment, the correct cloaking sequence, and a data pick fine as the few seconds she might have before detection. Things slipped into alignment, and Petal let her finger twitch.

The screen froze momentarily, but not before she saw the piggyback signal picking up each tech's teleport work, the licenses that allowed the transfer, and Dunphries' worm trail hidden amongst the garbage commands that hid the breach. Much of HRO lay bare to him, or whoever he let in. They could have done anything ... embezzled funds, stolen donor identities, sold HRO's tech right out from under them ... or rerouted the extractees to send them who knew where.

A message box popped up on Petal's terminal.

"Please come to my office," Dunphries had typed.

Petal noted her location in the system, pocketed the mem stick, shut down her terminal, and with a quick, bracing breath went to face Dunphries.

She had seen enough federal agents in relief centers to recognize that two of them were sitting in Dunphries' office when she entered. With an effort she kept walking inside. Her mind raced with possibilities. Before she could speak, one of the agents approached her.

"Do you know this girl?" he asked, holding a photo of the Indonesian toddler up at her eye level.

"Yes, of course. But—" Petal began.

"You should." The agent looked at her with disgust. "Since you sent her there. You look confused. I guess you don't pay attention to where they end up. This photo is from Fun Things, one of the blackest holes in the darknet."

"I didn't send her anywhere. I lost her before—"

"Petal Scott, you're under arrest for kidnapping, conspiracy, corruption of a minor, and sex trafficking."

"What?! No! I didn't do that! None of that! Dunphries! He was involved; not me. I—" Petal turned to face her accuser. And she found herself on her knees, unable to move. She fell to the floor, the taser wires now visible.

She felt the full weight of the man on her back as he

ground his knee between her shoulder blades and cuffed her. The other agent pulled her up to her feet. She saw the mem stick on the ground.

There! Look at that! At first she didn't realize that they couldn't hear her. The taser had left her only able to mumble and pant for her next breath. Dunphries stepped on the mem stick. He stared into space as they pulled her out of HRO and dumped her into the back of their vehicle.

The lockup stank of desperation, body odor, and the urine of a homeless woman camped out in the corner of the cell. Petal ached where they had tasered her and winced from a tender spot on her back whenever she moved. She couldn't imagine a worse day.

It came when the court deemed her a flight risk and sent her to the Salem Federal Facility for Women.

She spent the first week crying, cultivating a migraine that left her curled up on the thin mattress, shielding her eyes from the fluorescents that lit up the cell all day and most of the night. Intermittently, she rushed to the toilet in the corner and vomited as her body tried to acclimate to the food and her soul to the pain it now bore. Her cellmate, a tall brunette with a thick Slavic accent, ignored Petal as best she could, but on the eighth day when the smell had coated every surface in the room, she spoke.

"Enough," the woman said. "It stinks. Stop it." Petal heard her take a few steps. "Stop retching up what got you here and start dealing with where you are."

Petal felt something small land behind her and turned to find a foil packet of antacids.

"For your stomach. Otherwise you'll have to go to the infirmary. You won't like the guards there."

Petal raised her gaze to look the woman in the face.

"I am Kasia," she said.

Petal started to unfold herself and reached for the packet. “Thank you. I’m Petal.”

“Hm. I’d suggest using your surname here. The C.O. said it was ... Smith?”

“Scott. Why won’t I like the guards?” Petal asked.

“They believe they should be paid for the privilege of medical attention. They prefer flesh as payment.” Kasia walked back to her bunk and sat. “The world loves its skin trade.”

“Is that why you’re here?” Petal asked.

“No, Scott. But I’ve done that time. Not you, though. I can tell.”

“How?” Petal asked.

Kasia chuckled, ignored the question. “What did you do outside?”

“Teleport tech.”

Kasia hummed. “You must have done well for yourself then. There are so many things people want relocated into their possession.”

“Not like that. I worked for an NGO, a—”

“I know what an NGO is,” Kasia said.

“You’d be surprised.”

“Rarely,” Kasia responded.

That night Petal slept. She began to eat her meals, to speak with the other women, to accept the reality she found herself in. But she also fought for her freedom, cleaning out her bank account to pay lawyers and keep up payments on her tiny house. With the rest of her savings, she arranged for her personal rig to be boxed and stored. She would get out, she told herself.

In the meantime Petal created a routine. After the exercise allotment, enduring inspections, and picking her way through the day’s dangers, she returned to her cell where she wrote code by hand and listened to Kasia’s stories of the bumpy road from Plotzyk to Portland by way of every dark alley imaginable.

"I was raised in crime," Kasia said from her bunk, a crossword in her hand. "So you see, I was cultivated, but most people are corrupted," Kasia said. "An easier process than you might imagine. Where there is virtue, vice lurks."

Petal looked away from the code and up at her cellmate. Kasia seemed to contemplate something and spoke again, this time softly.

"For instance ... you use the tech to help people; others want to help themselves. If one can pay, it's a lot easier to steal a girl tripping through the black than one off the street. And what better girl than one who can't be traced, a girl who might be dead anyway? There are men that do this, who gather their resources for it, like—" Kasia said.

"Like the people who crowdfund HRO's rescues," Petal finished.

"I was going to say wolves. These wolves stole the virtuous model and twisted it to their purposes. They call themselves 'voiders'. 'To be avoided,' we girls used to say," Kasia said with a tight, angry smile.

The loss of her last bit of naiveté burdened Petal. Her head drooped with the weight of this new knowledge, all the way down to the tabletop. She sat with her eyes closed.

"Of course. Thank you, K," she said quietly.

In time Petal's eyes opened. The florescent light overhead looked brighter, the shadows it created, deeper. Underneath the table, at the page's corners, even outlining her hands—the gloom behind everything, emboldened, emerged. It called to her.

Would it swallow her finally? Do what the fire and the work had not? If it did, what would become of the people so easily lost ... and the perpetrators who, for her, could easily be found? She picked her head up wearily. As she did, the shadows shifted. Petal paused in mid-motion. Even shadows can be displaced.

"Leave nothing up to the judges," she whispered.

Petal looked at the code, and a new, bolder imperative

clicked into place. She reached for a fresh sheet of paper and began again, hand flying across the page to capture her rushing thoughts.

Petal spent 28 months sharpening her skills. It took those two years and a spring for the court to find the prosecutor had insufficient evidence to convict. Kasia was impressed. She said Petal must have some kind of luck to get out at all—even if Petal's lawyers said the arrest ruined her professional reputation. Petal didn't believe in luck, only in doing. At work she used to say she made other people's luck; now she understood how short the distance to misfortune. She had just spent 28 months calculating it exactly.

Her first day out Petal sprung her rig from cold storage. Two years of lost updates would slow her down. It would mean at least a week of getting back up to speed: Petal relished the thought.

Her first crooked job came easily. She sat in the one-bedroom house she stopped calling home after her second HRO assignment abroad and logged into the darknet with the rig she'd retrofitted specifically for the task. The darknet's layout looked unnecessarily opaque and seedy—someone's idea of what elicit should look like—all choppy fonts and DOS aesthetics. She moved to a search page to retrieve "trafficking" results. She'd specified "art trafficking" to save herself from images she wouldn't be able to forget. She planned on tracking the voiders later, and in some way that wouldn't keep her up at night. Kasia had assured her that identities were cheap here, and each sex trafficking site kept a list of its patrons complete with all chip and location info hacked back to their origin from the moment they logged on. Because of it, Petal would have to spend her first payment on a specialized sub-rig invisible to anyone but her. If she hadn't already had her own chip removed, she would have spent her second payment on that, but now she could put that money to better use.

The second "trafficking" hit provided the results she wanted. She found a job board of sorts and posted her skills and experience. Soon after, she proved it with a series of tests. After a long vet process her reply came back in flashing chartreuse characters.

"You're hired," it read. "Ready to get to work?"

Petal assented. An icon appeared at the corner of her screen. When she motioned it open a building schematic appeared, and Petal prepared to extract a Degas from a vault in Tel Aviv. The job paid a year's salary.

With her third deposit she bought a backdoor key into HRO's systems. There she set her long-honed algorithm loose. It took longer than she had anticipated, but in five minutes the uplink completed: she had full access to HRO's systems and had fully cloaked her actions. Her second screen filled with live natural disaster info: latitude, longitude, magnitude, description, and estimates of the number affected. She pressed her list of coordinates onto the edge of the screen. Next she searched the HR records. Dunphries had been terminated, the stated reason: a statistically unacceptable string of lost souls on his watch, all attributed to user error and equipment failure. In another module she found that none of the lost extractees had been located—even those that were chipped. The stolen girl had no chip. Petal couldn't find her because of it, but maybe she could locate some of these girls who were—perhaps still are—chipped. She saved the necessary info down to her terminal in case she lost the connection and navigated to the teleport module.

Thunder rumbled overhead as Petal set about locating and extracting the lost souls from their unnatural disasters. She'd lost none of her speed on the controls; in fact she moved faster now. She didn't know if the simpler tasks or more compelling conditions spurred her. She found three women and two children in North America in a matter of minutes, the sixth not 500 miles away from where she sat. Petal engaged the CCTV hack app she'd received as an incentive for her latest job and waited for the arcs to align. At that instant she enacted the first extraction.

As the first foundling appeared outside a relief center, Petal watched her look around in terror and confusion. Dirt covered her skin and night gown, as if she had been unearthed. Even from a distance, she looked years older than the photo taken months before. Relief flooded into her expression. She lowered her hands, no longer needing to ward off whatever had been approaching. She jerked her head around the empty street and saw the relief center's sign. Without another glance, forward or back, she ran inside.

Petal stared at the space she'd been standing in, unable for the moment to think clearly or act. She blinked and saw the Indonesian girl's face. She extracted the other lost souls without taking the time to watch. As the last one arrived back in her hometown, Petal could only feel her heart thumping in her chest, her shoulders release.

An alert chimed on her rig. Petal's gaze slowly drifted up to the top monitor where it reported that a hurricane now scoured the Atlantic coast of Florida. Petal shifted at her terminal and with a sequence of graceful motions effortless as dance, she relocated the first selection of voiders into the eye wall of the storm.

Petal felt a vastness open in her, a laying out of possibilities and matrices that until now had not existed. Gauging her next move, she analyzed the shift.

Lopsided World

When Songo dropped his end of the world, Libanja's forearms trembled and the clouds over the east Manchurian highlands swooped down so suddenly that some villagers wondered what good deed had elevated them into the heavens.

In the west, cities crumbled. The concrete and steel could not hold the weight of the sky. So from British Columbia to Caracas, buildings became part of the sea. The flotsam shored up around Songo's giant body and the pole he still held.

On land, bodies were crushed into a dust that clung close to the ground, filling the survivors' lungs with a murk so thick they would have to evolve to survive.

So they did.

And Akongo's prophecy came true: men and women became lizards and lived life on their bellies.

In the west.

In the east, people searched for the reason behind the crooked sky. They did not know of Libanja. Her people had perished centuries ago; in their homeland the horizon slanted but bore no other clues. Even the god Akongo, who had given her and Songo the poles and placed him in the west and her in the east, had disappeared. But Libanja had been busy and so did not know. Neither she nor the survivors had anyone to explain the lopsided world.

So they made it up.

The lizards slept in the shade of the debris and sunned themselves on great outcroppings of stone. They mated and fought, much the same as ever, only now they did so in the three feet of space from ground to sky. The men and women who still had room to stand sometimes ferried out to the end of the world, East Africa, and dropped their jaws at what they found there.

When they got home they wondered whether to kill their tiny lizards or worship them.

In the peaks of the highlands, Libanja struggled to keep her footing. The sky swayed, pulled by the wind and her exhaustion. Sometimes she cried for her brother. Though the world had grown beneath her, Libanja only remembered Songo—how he looked just before he turned away from her, and she from him, and they made their way to opposite posts. Everything else has been mountains and the blue above her. She thought of his grave smile when she squared her shoulders and bent her knees against the burden.

When not thinking of Songo, Libanja watched splinters sprout down her pole.

For a time, the lopsided world continued as such.

When Libanja dropped her end of the world, the pole slivered beneath the weight. She'd ground the other end into a mountain. Above, the heavens creaked and groaned struggling to balance on the thin shaft.

Just after Libanja reached her brother, who was now a giant island in the middle of the North Pacific, the pole collapsed.

In the east, the survivors learned to live low to the ground, not sure if it was the beginning or end of their world.

The Taken

For all of the construction committee's planning, some details couldn't be replicated exactly. So the barracoons that housed the senatorial sons and daughters had approximately two more square feet of space than those historically built for transatlantic slaves. As more hooded figures were shoved into the cage, Kristen Burke, ignorant of the inaccuracy, felt no gratitude for this small luxury.

She had been the first. First to be stripped down to her thin cotton shirt and silk leggings. First to be branded with ND just below her ankle bone. First to have the tape and hood ripped off before they pushed her into the cage.

That was last night or maybe this morning. There were no clocks or natural light in the warehouse. She knew it hadn't been more than a day since the agent—or what she thought was an agent—led her into the idling car that was supposed to take her to her father. When she woke up, cotton-mouthed and head pounding, Senator Burke was not among the men dressed in military black who hustled her through the cold and into the warehouse door. She'd screamed through the tape over her mouth, but by then she was here with grim-faced people who seemed to expect her screams.

Now three women shared the cage with her, shivering and bleary-eyed. She recognized Margaret Eastland from her parents' dinner parties and Bridget Hardy from her mother's campaign commercials. Kristen couldn't place the young blonde girl who leaned on her ankle where they had burned her. Though tears slid down her face, Kristen paid the pain no mind.

The warehouse was loud. Gates slid open and closed. Men yelled a language she couldn't understand. Margaret Eastland kept screaming every few minutes, words garbled behind the tape still on her mouth. Somewhere out of sight, metal scraped against metal. Boxes hit floors, and behind all this more voices rose. Kristen couldn't see where they came from, but they never stopped or even paused in their monotonous roar. More than once she thought her ears had started bleeding from all the noise. She would wipe at them spastically, only for her hand to come back clean, save for the sheen of sweat.

She wished Eastland would shut up. Or that Bridget Hardy would speak again. They'd shared a few words when Bridget first arrived. As soon as they dumped her in, she started asking questions. Her blue eyes boring into Kristen's, she'd asked who she was, where had she come from, how long had she been there? Kristen Burke. Manhattan. She didn't know. Two men had scooped Bridget off the street in front of her Upper East Side apartment with the same story that got Kristen off the NYU campus and into a dark sedan. Everyone who was anyone knew Eastland kept a place in Murray Hill, so they'd probably taken her from there. Kristen would bet on the blonde girl, too. All Manhattan, all in the last day or two. All senators' daughters.

And sons: Five men filled the second cage.

Kristen didn't wonder who'd taken them. It was plain as the brand on her skin: "ND," New Dawn. Rumors about the group ricocheted from the news reports to the Senate Floor to conversation over martinis at Saul's Bistro. Of all the groups demanding reparations for slavery, none was more feared than New Dawn. They didn't want educational vouchers or free medical care like the other groups, they wanted everything—land redistribution, financial compensation, and stock in every conglom that had benefited from slavery. And even by 2024, that was all the conglomerations. Worse, New Dawn didn't believe in legislation or picketing or economic sanctions. They believed in results. The one and only press statement New Dawn ever issued said just that: "We believe in results." Those words perplexed people outside of political circles. It worried her father's camp. Like Kristen, they knew what it took to get results.

A man in a black mask sat on a low stool outside of Kristen's cage. He'd been staring at Margaret Eastland for the last few hours, the hours she'd spent screaming. Now he looked in Kristen's direction. He turned his eyes slowly, as if measuring each inch between them. Kristen's lip quivered, shivers turned to jolts as he turned his full attention on her. Like the dozen other men outside the cages, he was dressed in all black, a mesh mask obscuring his features. It was hard to tell his height, but he seemed big holding a long stun stick. He tapped it on the floor every few minutes, sending blue sparks dancing along the concrete. Kristen tried to look him in the eye, but the mask stopped her. It had an opalescent sheen, making it seem to float in front of his face. The Mask looked her up and down, stopping at her stomach, her breasts, her bent shoulders and sweaty face. The longer he looked, the more her throat tightened, the harder it became to breathe. She tried to distract herself, craning her neck to look into the men's cage, but her skin prickled with the weight of his stare. Kristen turned back, looked down at the scratches on her hands, the dirt under her fingernails. After thirty minutes she began to understand why Eastland screamed.

Somewhere inside the building a door slammed. Kristen jumped, jabbing her elbow into one of the bars. The Mask laughed at her, then fell silent, staring up at the landing behind the cages. For a moment, she could see the man beneath the mask, the reverence that smoothed out the tight lines around his mouth. She followed his gaze.

Phillip Tailor, New Dawn's leader, wore no mask; instead he donned a smile. Like the others, he wore black fatigues. In place of the mask, a pair of opaque glasses covered his eyes. A tall man, he towered over the cages, and Kristen felt a spell of vertigo. Tailor nodded acknowledgment at the man guarding Kristen's cage. Leaning gracefully over the railing, he surveyed the busy warehouse floor. Another Mask, much smaller than Tailor, walked up to him. The Mask said something in that gibberish language and, with another nod, Tailor was gone.

Abruptly, Eastland stopped screaming. The Mask returned to his original posture, leaving a trail of blue sparks as he slowly dragged the stun stick back to his side. Margaret Eastland slumped against the bars, fingers twitching the last of the voltage from her system. The blonde girl scurried farther away from the prone body, pinning Kristen into the corner. Kristen was grateful for the sweat pressed into her skin, grateful for someone to hold onto, and come between her and the apparition who scrutinized her, sparking blue intention across the floor.

Their captors were yelling more. Still holding the blonde girl, Kristen tried to follow one set of gibberish from man to man. The tone suggested commands, but she couldn't be sure. She looked toward the sound of a bodega gate coming down. This gate was much bigger and going up. The whole wall behind the barracoons recessed into its upper reaches and let dawn in. She smelled saltwater, heard distant traffic, and hoped for a moment. Maybe New Dawn had gotten their ransom. Maybe her father had arrived. Maybe someone would see them and send agents. Maybe, maybe.

Her brain stuttered at the sight of the gangplank. It could hardly take in the ship and open water beyond it. She opened her mouth to scream. Hours of sitting hadn't slowed the Mask. He lunged with precision, knocking over his stool. The stun stick passed through the barracoon's bars and touched Kristen's shoulder. Still clutching each other, she and the blonde girl shared the strong current.

Conscious, but unable to move, Kristen watched as her hand slipped from the tangle of blonde hair receding from her grasp. After New Dawn dragged the younger girl out, they pulled at Kristen's ankles. She felt the silk, then her skin, tear against the rough floor. When her head fell from the cage's lip and onto the concrete, she whimpered.

The Mask hovered close to her face, squinting at her. He reached down and pinched her ear. Hard. Her hand jumped. He grunted low in his throat, snatched her up by her armpits so that they were face to face. She heard him exchange a few words with someone. Another set of hands held her from behind, her head resting against a broad chest. Her gaze followed the other women being dragged out of the door and into the half-light—then out of her field of vision.

The man behind the mask peeled it up from the bottom, stopped just above his lips. A translation patch stuck to the mesh's underside. Now the gibberish made sense.

"Say goodbye to home," he said, his voice clear and deep without the conversion.

The hands behind her covered her mouth and lifted her away from the barracoon, toward the ship.

She was trying to remember the diagrams. All her life, she'd flipped past the Black History Month specials, those horrible images somebody should have forgotten by now. But now she wished she could remember. Then at least she would have some idea what the hold looked like. Maybe then she'd know where the blonde girl was and where they'd put the men. She could feel flesh, but the heat made it difficult to tell which was hers. The Masks hadn't been back down since they'd chained the captives to each other, and then the ship. And she'd been near unconsciousness then.

Someone coughed. Was that a man's cough or a woman's? Did it matter? Someone was awake. She tried to use her voice. When she heard it, it sounded like she'd been up for days, high on too much Mystique.

"Bridget?" she pleaded into the dark. "Margaret?"

"Matthew." The voice came from beneath her. "Matt Holleran. From Georgia."

Kristen saw a flash of a gangly red-headed boy with green eyes beaming out from an "Equality is Now!" poster. Senator Holleran and his family had posed for the short-lived campaign that was supposed to help end the call for reparations. She thought back to the faces in the men's cage. There. The one with the dark red beard. Broad-chested, head bent beneath the cage's low ceiling. Matthew Holleran.

"Blake Denning," a voice below her.

"Harry Anderson," and another.

"Preston Caleb," this one from above.

"Bridget Hardy," the skin on her left.

A high-pitched whisper from above, "Margaret Eastland."

"Chuck Lassiter," the skin on her right.

"Drew Ellison."

Captain Tailor watched the infrared images calling out their names. He tapped the screen, then turned down the volume. Should feed them soon. No, just water, he corrected himself. He'd been battling how many inaccuracies to allow, trying to find the balance between highlighting their advantages and introducing them to the Middle Passage's suffering, so that they could in turn introduce the White world. Though he and his crew were perpetrating one of the most ambitious experiments in the Rep War campaign, he had to maintain parameters. Already, he worried about the Examples' advantages: a shared language, a smaller group, the faster voyage, and of course, all the moral prerogatives: no rape, no dying, limited physical abuse. But he aimed to get the majority into their heads and hopefully their hearts through the body. Identity politics infused with psychological warfare. He knew the formula would get results. He had to remain vigilant if they were to be the right results.

Shireen walked into the surveillance room, still talking on her handheld.

"What's the final count on that?" she sighed, thanked the person on the other line and hung up. She walked toward Tailor, slipping the handheld into her bulky jacket.

"Fifteen dead at the Baltimore demonstration though they're only reporting them as injuries. Over 300 arrests."

"What about Tuscaloosa and DC?" he asked.

She sat down in the chair next to Captain Tailor.

"The Representatives in Tuscaloosa never stopped walking, just got in their transports and bolted. And the PFC postponed the March in DC." She pulled the rolled-up mesh fabric down to her ears. "It's cold in here."

"Again." He answered to both statements. "How many postponements does that make?"

"Three. This time something about one of the organizer's connections to the Court of International Trade muddying the waters."

He laughed. "Once again, nonviolent proves itself nonviable."

Shireen fell silent. They'd always disagreed on this point. He knew that she believed a happy medium existed between the extremes; that she'd signed up for this project to protect the Examples, though Monitor was her official title, and, on the ship, First Mate. That title must have rankled her feminist leanings. But that's exactly why Tailor needed her: Shireen didn't say "yes" unless she meant it.

Tailor stood and walked over to the heart and blood pressure monitors that made up the center wall. He tore off hard copies of the latest readings and filed them away, made sure the digifiles were simultaneously saving and transmitting to the processors stateside.

It felt good to stand; he'd been at the monitors for nearly two hours, making notes for the first draft of his press statement. He stretched his arms toward the ceiling, looked out the window at the crew taking in the fresh night air. Latrell shared a cigarette with TwoTone. Their light jackets flapped in the breeze, as the smoke swirled around the bill of TwoTone's ever-present cap. Good men, those. They knew enough not to ask questions. He wouldn't have to worry about them; they would do the job and take the freedom offered in Ghana, leave all the restrictions on felons behind and live as full men again. His attention to the details was just as much for this New Dawn crew as for the nine below. The voyage would change them just as profoundly.

He turned back to Shireen who sat, jaw tensed, looking at the surveillance monitors.

"Should we feed them now?"

"Yes," she answered. "I'll go with TwoTone."

"I'll go with you two," Tailor answered. He retrieved a mask from the top of the monitor banks.

Shireen looked at him quizzically.

"Research," he answered to the unspoken question.

Captain Tailor and Shireen collected the stocky man outside. All three pulled their masks down, opalescence shimmering in the moonlight, as they walked.

The hold stank. Even with the masks' air filters, a level of the stench still entered Tailor's nose—a sharp unpleasantness that reached past technology to give him the impression of feces, urine, and vomit. It smelled like the Rep War: everything let go after being pent up too long. Yes, he knew that smell.

Walking past the containers of food and medicines New Dawn would bring onto the shores of West Africa, they reached the back corner where the nine lay, three by three, in a space designed for two industrial sinks. Shireen added powdered protein to the cornmeal mush and handed it to TwoTone who did the water and food detail. Captain Tailor stood nearby, taking notes on a legal pad. He stepped closer and hovered near the middle tier. Shireen climbed atop the structure and searched for an ankle to spray with the anti-biotic salve. Tailor heard her sigh; she turned and looked at him, her expression unreadable. She told TwoTone to give everyone extra water. Shireen's words came out in Icelandic. With the trans link in his ear TwoTone understood well enough. After the training, time in the warehouse setting things up and the sea, they could both probably speak the strange language without the aid of trans patches. At first Shireen had questioned Tailor about his "odd choice", but now he was sure she understood: who could understand Icelandic? Most people couldn't even recognize it.

Kristen dreamt of the sky. Its light gray tones bobbed by, the sun still hidden in dawn's hues: not the sunset sky of her trip to Bali or the bright blue receding and advancing of her childhood swing, not even the rare red sunrise on the Hudson after a long night of cocktails and conversation. She dreamt of the last sky she saw, bobbing above, as her head bumped on the slats of the pier.

Up on deck, the sky was clearer than Kristen had dreamt it. She kept her eyes on it as she stumbled up and down the small deck. She didn't want to look at the men, the men without their masks. They barked commands in that strange language, though their waving hands made their meaning clear enough. Here. Go Here. Faster. Faster. Stop. Get Back. Right Now. Do It Again.

She didn't want to see the others from the hold either. If they could just not look at each other, one day they might be able to see one another without the memory. Kristen doubted that "one day" would ever come. Apparently, New Dawn didn't care if she and the others saw their faces. So the men would probably kill them out here on the open sea. They believed in results.

When they had to go back to the hold, Kristen missed the light.

If left in its grasp too long, the dark crawls over you and molds you into something unrecognizable. Already Kristen's back had changed shape. Fluid filled her lungs. Her skin had become a separate animal that she tried to fight off. She'd been in the dark for five days.

That night the crew came down to choose their bedwarmers. Tailor picked Kristen.

When the two men who'd brought her up took off the blindfold, Tailor was already seated at a small table, a pitcher of amber-colored liquid at his elbow. The room was small. No more than a cot bolted to the floor and the table. Tailor took the tail of the chain around her wrists from one of the crewmen and bid them good night. As soon as they were gone, he pulled the chain roughly, causing her to stumble closer to the cot. Wrapping the chain around the cot leg, he produced a small lock that he secured to the couplings, and chained her legs to the bottom of the cot.

Tailor, winded, pulled up a chair and posed a question.

"Imagine no one had tended to your brand. How do you think it would look now? How much pain would you be in?"

Kristen didn't answer. Could hardly breathe. Tailor inclined his head slightly and continued.

"Imagine that there were 190 of you instead of nine. What do you think it would smell like? How many would be dying?"

Silence.

"Imagine that you'd had to walk the forty miles between

where we captured you and the warehouse. How close to death would you have been in your high heels and silk pajamas?"

Rage moved through her. She bucked in the chains, spraining her wrist, bruising her ankles. She called him every name she could think of. Names she didn't know that she knew. She screamed her throat raw and then lay glaring at him, breath shooting out in short bursts.

Tailor looked at her, smiling a little. Then asked another question.

He went on like that until the sun came up. Just before he called the crewmen to lead her back into the hold he said:

"Now imagine that I had raped you."

The well of tears that had threatened to spill all night, came brimming over Kristen's lids. She leaned against the doorframe, head bowed, trying to hide her face from him.

"Next time," he said, looking at her intently, "if you do what I want, you can have some of the peach juice. It's your favorite, no?"

On the way back to the hold, the crewmen walked a full foot in front of Kristen. They held her chain away from their bodies and looked down at the floor or out at sea. At the entrance they waited for Kristen to walk through, careful not to touch her.

She was the last one to be brought back to the hold. Eight shadows filled the bank between the ceiling and floor. They hardly moved, didn't speak, though she could hear one of the men on the top row whimpering. One crewman waited at the entrance while the other dragged the chain across the planks and locked Kristen back in place. The two left silently, footfalls heavy and slow.

The wood beneath Kristen creaked in time to the waves, but there were no human sounds, not from the crew above or the ones down below. It was as if a spell had been cast over everyone on the ship, and now each person lie quietly trying to remember how they'd become so afflicted. Kristen supposed this because she, herself, could think of nothing else.

It was enough that her mind was working again. In the last few days it had abandoned her for long stretches of time, capable of nothing more than the automatic functions of pumping her heart and breathing. Kristen would wait, ambivalent about the return of her awareness. Gradually, it let her hear the sound of scurrying after a long stretch of silence. When she could feel the cold moisture pooled under her buttocks, she knew it had returned. For better or for worse.

Later, she heard the hold door open. Someone above her keened a quick note of terror. She watched as a shaft of light knifed through the dark, growing larger and brighter. Chains knocked against wood as the captives shifted, trying to curl away.

The door closed. When Kristen's eyes adjusted, four of the crewmen stood at her feet. They'd already unlocked the men on the bottom row; now they worked on her manacles.

Up on deck, the captives huddled near each other. The remnants of their clothes hung at odd angles. All the silk that had once covered Kristen's back was worn away, leaving only deep scratches on her reddened skin. She looked better than most of the other women. The crew kept their distance. No one shouted for dancing or prodded them with the short end of a stun stick. A half dozen crewmen stood against the railing, staring out into the sea. Others dragged fire hoses into the hold to blast out its offal. These were the same men who had hauled the women and two of the men away last night, their shouts louder than the captives' pleas; today, they looked stooped, a little less full.

~

"Bedwarmers, Phillip!" Shireen stood in the middle of the monitor room, arms across her chest, glaring at Captain Tailor.

"It's good to finally hear you call me by my first name, Shireen."

She clenched her teeth until a solid square of tread emerged from the corners of her jaw.

"You watched the monitors all night. Did anything happen?" he asked.

"Hell yes, something happened: you went too far."

"Too far?" Tailor flared with his own anger now; his voice went quiet and steady. "This is nothing! A few questions and an uncomfortable night at the foot of someone's bed. Why, Latrell even gave up his bed! Too far? They're not children. They're not dying. This is just a taste of suffering. A taste! They get to go free at the end, Shireen. Their children will be free. Their minds will be free. They won't work a single day. Mark my words: no one will ever deny them their due. Not far enough perhaps, but not nearly too far."

Kristen heard Tailor's voice and flinched, jerked her head toward the railing. Two of the male captives stared at her. When Kristen saw how the men looked at her, she knew she had become part of their nightmare. And they would never remember her any other way.

Tailor sent for her. He shackled her to the table, hands pulled down into her lap by a chain looped under the seat, through the back of the chair, and around her waist. Kristen barely resisted. Fatigue had most of her; the rest stared at the camera and tripod pointed at the small cot in the corner of the room. Tailor pushed her up to the table and placed the pitcher of peach juice below her chin. Kristen's nose worked independently of the rest of her, pulling deep breaths of peach into her mouth and chest. Captain Tailor sat down opposite her. He crossed his legs loosely at the ankle.

She eyed the video camera over his shoulder, a hot knot of foreboding forming in her stomach. She wanted to believe the camera had been there the last time but knew it had not. Tailor's last words to her echoed in her memory. Between them, her pain, abject hunger, and the cold gusting around the edge of the door, it was all she could do to stay conscious—never mind sane.

"Kristen—" Captain Tailor looked directly at her, his tone even.

For twenty-two years, Kristen, Senator Burke's daughter, answered when someone called her name. The new Kristen, woman snatched from her native soil, cried when she heard her name for the first time. She made no sound, only shook with her pain. Every other heartbeat she gasped for breath. Her hands hung loosely in her lap, head dropped straight down into her chest.

Captain Tailor reached behind him to turn the camera around. And started his questioning.

Kristen broke before the agents came, even before they'd reached the Tropic of Cancer. She told Tailor all the answers to his questions. All the ways her passage differed, bettered. Listed all the things she didn't go through, mentioned the medical care she'd received. Learned his brutal lesson. Tailor had to reload the camera she talked so much. In between answers, she guzzled from the goblet of amber-colored liquid. The juice tasted sweet, better than Kristen remembered.

In the end, Tailor threw away his own draft and broadcast Kristen Burke—dirty, ragged, and grateful—as his statement.

Publishable Regrets

This is *Sincerely*'s last day of publication. I thank The Toledo Beacon for allowing us this space and being a bridge for 12 amazing years. Through the cynicism and the lawsuits, the editorial board stood by me, and for this forum's right to exist. The Beacon lent us their credibility when we had none of our own. I will always be grateful, and I know that the loved ones of those whose secrets were shared here feel the same.

More than a couple of police departments have also grudgingly acknowledged our work. I'm writing this message in part so it's clear we've left of our own free will—and not because skeptics proved us wrong or ran us out.

Sincerely is not and never was fiction. We were the first, but are no longer the only, sincere forum for the deceased to share their secrets, own up to their shames, and free themselves so that they and the living they left behind find peace.

To date, we have published 596 posthumous confessions, assisted in the resolution of 46 crimes, and saved three lives.

As important as this work is, it was never what I intended to do with my life or my career. But like the regrets that filled this page, intention had little to do with where I ended up.

I started here at the Beacon, green and determined. I wanted to emulate my journalistic heroes and investigate the underside of Northwest Ohio, as ridiculous as that sounds now. But coming from tiny Woodmere, to me, Toledo was an accessible and, frankly, preferable Gotham. I got the job right out of college because I'd work for half what the position should pay—that was still more than the Beacon could afford, so I took a third. I started with the obits, worked my way up to the police blotter, and finally began to assist with the actual crime beat—interviewing victims, building agency contacts, finding sources. I was in heaven. No one could tell me researching the annual property damage caused by joyriding kids wasn't the best way to spend a Saturday night.

The years went by. I paid my dues, and I was lucky enough that that worked. Finally, the day came: My editor sent me on A Big Story. I didn't know then that that story would come to eclipse my life.

It's old news now: the Lagrange hostage standoff, the wild shot that caught me looking the wrong way and how I heard the first spirit as I slipped in my blood to the ground. Many of you have already heard that she followed me for weeks, and how, when I heard the second voice, I almost ran off the road. I told that story during my only interview 11 years ago. I've heard it repeated back to me numerous times, twisted and tinted, until I hardly recognized it.

That's the thing about stories; they have a life of their own.

When it started, I didn't tell anyone what was going on, not until the O-T Bottle Plant fire. Reluctantly, I covered the story—mostly because I couldn't think of a way out of it. While I waited to talk to a company spokesperson in an adjacent lot crowded with fire engines, ambulances, and emergency personnel, I heard a gruff voice grieving in the darkness. I offered a few words of comfort and turned to see if he had heard me. Behind me, I saw only the fire engines' flashing lights, and I realized my mistake too late.

Of the fifty-nine people who perished in the fire,

twenty-six souls followed me home that night.

They would not let me be. They found me in the dark: when I tried to sleep, on night roads that stretched from the office to home, while I sat on the front stairs wondering how long it took to lose one's grip on reality. The voices swelled into a chorus, overwhelming my own thoughts, but somehow also endearing them to me.

They were so pure in their desires and singular in their purpose. They only wanted to unburden themselves, as do we all.

The spirits who lingered with me did not threaten me to get their way. They just stayed with me, and that was enough. They kept me enveloped in their sadness, the sadness of where they had gone wrong in their lives and who had paid for their mistakes. I could hear their laments—so they wouldn't leave. But I was not really who they wanted to speak to. Luckily this medium had a medium.

I pitched the idea to my editor, the incomparable Sydney Grace. I didn't use full names or tell him at first where the entries came from. I said it could be the Beacon's version of Lonely Hearts or Missed Connections, but more engaging. With hopes of selling more papers, he gave us a chance, never called it journalism, and placed us between the classifieds and the obituaries. He called it the "Dead Zone." I hid my smirk.

It took a while to find our audience. One particularly helpful reader, Tyler2000, informed us that we'd misspelled "Utter Fiction" in the section header (Full disclosure—I did once toy with calling the section "Publishable Regrets"). Questionable wit aside, I remember that comment because a man named Tyler died of pleurisy two years later and came coughing to me soon after. He spent the entire month of April asking me to tell his ex-wife that cheating on her was the dumbest, worst thing he had ever done in his whole 73-cent life. He said it just that way, so that's how I wrote it up. Three days after publication, I received a package with a single dollar bill inside. On it read, "Tell Tyler it's too late to change, so here's a refund." When I told Tyler the story and lay the dollar bill on the table in front of me, his bright laughter filled the room until it broke free, leaving only a welcome sliver of silence where he had once been.

I know that a lot of people don't believe any of this. I envy your disbelief. I have not had that luxury for years. I miss it—perhaps most when I'm jolted awake in the middle of the night by the cold pang of someone else's dread, my eyes already watering from the guilt they reek of when they find me. I've no choice but to take a sip of water from the glass I keep on my bedside table for such occasions and open my laptop to capture what they dictate.

I'll be relieved when it's over. I'm sure that fatigue has influenced my decision. I'm OK with that. It will not trouble me, not now or when I'm gone. They have taught me that.

In fact, this is my first regret since the day I accepted I was not crazy. They've simplified things for me. I will not be haunted by what I have or have not done.

My dreams are not adventurous or lavish by many people's standards, but they are mine, and I have lived them, mostly.

So today we publish our first and only entry from a living person. And that is my entry, these words, this regret: I will no longer be able to bring you these confessions. To live as I now must, I can't stay here, with you, the fine people of this community in the warmest corner of Toledo.

I wanted to be the one to tell you. The dead already know, and they have lodged their complaint. Strangely, they think the silent treatment a fitting punishment. After all this time, they may be right.

Lately I can hear myself breathing before I fall asleep. They let me lie alone in the dark—no more mumbled lullabies, no more comforting cacophony.

Now there is only what burns in me. And because of it we are so much more the same.

I hope when I find myself in that final darkness, even before I see the afterlife that the dead have been unable to describe, I will hear their chorus again, and I'll know that I've been forgiven.

Evelyn Wright

Sugar Hill

There are six rats for every person in New York City. There are also three fairies, two Hathors, and an indeterminate, but increasing, number of haints. Lan Ts'ai-Ho is the only Immortal of ancient China. Though tonight may be a bad night, she lives in the city for the pleasure of it, and to watch moments like this free from the pesky interference of clouds:

A blackened stage, six inches above the dance floor. A tight spotlight lifts one image from the dark: silver-purple polish pressed into cocoa toes floating beneath black straps of sandal. The image catches Ts'ai-Ho and holds her there, halfway between the club's entrance and the restroom. She inhales slowly, her eyes narrowed in appreciation. Slow Spanish guitar begins to roll from the speakers. The spotlight widens and reveals Ms. Ter Ri perched on a barstool, her lips just beginning to hold the first notes of Annie Lennox's "A Thousand Beautiful Things."

Ms. Ter Ri looks splendid. Her dark skin glistens beneath the eggplant evening gown that hugs her narrow waist, dives down her chest, and comes to a point under the deep cleft of cleavage. Even in this club it's hard for the crowd to believe Ms. Ter Ri is pre-operative and thus, by the crudest definition, still a man.

Ts'ai-Ho knows better. She's lived hundreds of years dressed as a woman and sounding like a man. Still, the diva's performance is so stunning that Ts'ai-Ho almost forgets about Doren and why she came here. Then Doren's clear voice echoes in her mind, *I'm through, sick of this world,* and Ts'ai-Ho continues toward the bathroom to seek out the haint, Carl, who spends his days haunting his descendents on 149th and St. Nick and his nights peering up from the floor drain in this club's restroom.

When Ts'ai-Ho finally waits out the line and enters one of the unisex bathrooms, it smells like Carl, old and piss-soaked. Ts'ai-Ho stands near the corner of the small room, hands clasped in front of her. She whispers the haint's name until he slides up from the floor, his body bottlenecking out of the small drain.

"Well, if it ain't *La Dee Da*," Carl says, his head cocking with each syllable.

Ts'ai-Ho turns the corners of her mouth up a centimeter, stares at Carl until he's uncomfortable.

"Well, what you want? I know you didn't come for the scenery," he says.

"Where's Doren?" she asks. Carl jumps slightly at the sound of her voice, still shaken by its bass tones after all this time. He recovers quickly.

"You don't know where your friend's at?"

"Do you know or not?"

"Did you try Brooklyn?" he asks.

"All the fairies are gone from the gardens, botanical or otherwise. The museum's fetish dolls have taken dominion."

Carl turns his nose up.

"Dolls? What kind of dolls?"

"The spirits inside them, I said."

"No, you didn't."

"Carl," Tsai-Ho pauses, taps one finger, lowers her voice an octave. "Where is Doren?"

"Where you staying now?" Carl asks.

Ts'ai-Ho's lips purse slightly. She begins to repeat her question.

"Because," Carl cuts her off, "if you ever bothered to find out, you'd know he stays in Sugar Hill, just down the street from you, just down the street from here. He's been there for months."

Now it's Ts'ai-Ho's turn to jump. Could she and Doren have drifted so far apart that he could live so close without her knowing? A decade ago it would have been impossible, but time has deposited them on different shores. She, the ancient, gravitated to the present, and he, a third generation city-born fairy, has hankered for a past only spied in the pages of secondhand books.

She almost hadn't recognized Doren's voice on the answering machine. I'm through, sick of this world and its fucked-up stressed-to-press issues. The convent fairies are useless, well, fairies, sand blind them and god blast them. And I, Doren of the Dell, am Audi 5000 with big ups to the Boogie Down and Ballyheighe Bay.

Yes, they could have drifted that far.

Sharp raps on the restroom door.

Carl sidesteps into the wall and is gone before she can thank him or say anything at all.

She exits the restroom, glaring at the young man who rushes past her. Outside the show continues, but the diva has left the stage. Her replacement is unremarkable.

The moon meets Ts'ai-Ho at the top of the stairs. The dim streetlights that line St. Nicholas Avenue resonate the same pale yellow. Merengue rolls down the block, its epicenter a polished SUV in a line of double-parked cars. Teenagers gather around entranceways. Two bodegas blast bright light onto the sidewalk where a few gather and many more pass. Ts'ai-Ho moves confidently through her neighbors, a rare Asian face on a Black and brown block. Traffic flares in intermittent eruptions of horns; tail- and headlights flash. While Ts'ai-Ho hurries to save her friend, Saturday night keeps rolling down Sugar Hill.

As she nears Convent Avenue, the night grows quieter,

darker. Even before she rounds the corner to Convent, she squints, looking for fairies.

Though the street has the singular distinction of being the only stretch of green through the busy neighborhood, it's still a far cry from a glen or even the botanical gardens that fairy bands have inhabited in recent decades.

She stands still in the relative darkness, searching with her gaze. There, near the closest stoop: a glimmer of iridescent wings against denim. Ts'ai-Ho walks over, crouches at the edge of the sidewalk.

"Doren?" she asks. "Is that you?"

The fairy walks a few steps toward her, clothed in denim swatches from head to foot. It's not Doren.

"'Sup, Mami?" He's been drinking; his cheeks are so rosy that he almost glows in the dark.

"Have you seen Doren?" Ts'ai-Ho asks.

"You after that back-to-nature trick? For real though, Doren ain't shit. You need to bring that over here." He sweeps his right hand toward his crotch, nods on the last word.

Ts'ai-Ho clenches her jaw.

"I don't have time to play with you, fairy. I need to find Doren. Now."

"Damn, it's like that? You faded? I get horny as hell when I'm high."

Ts'ai-Ho sucks her teeth and stands up, looking for a sane fairy to speak with.

"Where is everyone?" she asks, already stepping away from the drunken fairy.

"Shit, it's Saturday night. They out getting they life."

As Ts'ai-Ho crosses the street, the fairy yells, "Yo, you ever want some real love, get at me!"

Ts'ai-Ho takes the steps up to her apartment two at a time. She mounts the landing outside her door, unlocks it, and enters. The door closes loudly behind her.

Ts'ai-Ho flips her shoes off in the hallway. They land cockeyed, close to the low shelf where they usually rest. She walks past the kitchen and the second bedroom, straight through to the back of the apartment where the answering machine sits atop an antique table, filigreed by Doren's light touch. Though she sees she has no messages, Ts'ai-Ho walks closer to the answering machine, willing the red light to blink. It does not.

Outside, a siren wails past, leaving an undertone of merengue in its wake.

For the first time Ts'ai-Ho misses the gods, who, for a song, might do her bidding. Her songs are so strong that the gods themselves granted her forever life just so they could hear her play. She looks to the dusty case in the corner that holds her flute. She knows if she opens it she will find the wood smooth and glossy from use, the mouthpiece shaped to the contour of her lips. She knows if she opens her mouth, the song will be just as strong, strong enough to take her out of this moment. But she doesn't open it. Instead, she sits on the couch and tries to decide what to do.

On the chest against her bare feet, a shard of yellow catches her eye. Ts'ai-Ho moves the piece of paper covering it, and a slight hush of wind escapes her lips. She's nearly forgotten the small yellow box with its runes and etched lid. She removes the lid and pulls the delicate dolls out by the tips of her fingernails.

Doren gave her the worry babies a year into their friendship. Even after he told her the name she didn't understand what to do with the small thread-covered figures inside the bright box. He explained that she should pull one out when she needed it. When she asked why, he answered, "So you don't have to worry, baby."

As Ts'ai-Ho places each one of the dolls on the edge of the chest, she sings a soft song to Doren, hoping that he hears.

~

In the four years since she has seen Doren—the actual Doren: thick black hair, dreaming blue eyes—Ts'ai-Ho has never believed that she would not see him again. This new possibility hovers over the worry babies and seeps into the thread.

When she heard his message this afternoon, Ts'ai-Ho had thought Doren was just throwing glamour. Once, glamour had dazzled her.

On the day they met, Ts'ai-Ho sat in the conservatory of the Botanical Gardens, playing her flute in solitude. The other patrons had deserted the building as closing time drew near. Ts'ai-Ho and her best friend, the flute, made the most of the quiet. Doren interrupted their solitude. He trundled in, a giant red tortoise that dragged its shell across the ground in long, loud scrapes. Ts'ai-Ho had stopped and stared. The tortoise Doren stared back, inclined his head, and explained: *Fairies front and call it glamour*. She had laughed into her flute—tickled as much by the sight of the widening grin on the tortoise's face as much as the thought of fairies calling their shape-shifting glamour at a time when humans did the same.

That night Doren introduced Ts'ai-Ho to the deeper layer of life pulsing through the flora. She saw Asrai transform from water trapped in petals to tiny women with long limbs calling to each other from the edges of flowers; watched as trows danced; heard the soft plop of water fairies lighting across the stream.

"This is New York City," Doren told her as they walked. The moon lit him up like an earth-born star. "There are as many secret places as there are secrets and beings to keep them. Fairyland is just one. And only in the Bronx. I hear they got some sick shit in Brooklyn."

For years Doren and Ts'ai-Ho watched the city change. From rooftops, park benches, and tree lines they saw whole nations emigrate from one borough to another. They picked up Nigerian and brogue in the streets, dusted them off, and exchanged them for Bangladeshi. Ts'ai-Ho's forty years in the city had been as exciting as four centuries on the Penglai, where the same seven immortals made for limited change. She'd found exactly what she wanted in New York. When she found Doren, she had someone to share it with. For a time he and Ts'ai-Ho were so close that they ran right up to the edges of each other. Little wonder then that Ts'ai-Ho didn't understand when Doren began to covet the "purity" of the old world.

The argument started when Ts'ai-Ho asked what Doren meant by "pure."

"Untainted, of course. Take fairies, who you see when you come to visit me—those aren't fairies," he said.

Because fairies are tricky and Doren in particular had a philosophical bent to boot, Ts'ai-Ho listened, expecting a punch line or at least a sharp turn away from idiocy. He continued.

"Fairies live in glens. Not in subway tunnels or the projects you call botanical gardens." He puffed up in anger. "They make mischief; they don't get wit' bitches."

Doren grew larger with each sentence.

"Fairies don't live in constant fear of rats or have to negotiate with them to take a fucking piss in the bushes!" he said.

Ts'ai-Ho cocked her head and hummed.

"Doren, I think perhaps—"

"No, Tsai, I'm telling you. I've got this—"

"All figured out?" Ts'ai-Ho said.

Doren, now half her height, turned to Ts'ai-Ho, changed his tone to match the tinge of derision in her comment.

"No, not all figured out," he paused. "Got an answer for everything, huh? This is my day in and day out. Trust, it ain't pretty, and it ain't pure. This is what I know, Ts'ai. You know your 1500, 1600 years, but I know these 500 blocks." Doren was pacing now, running a rut in the hardwood as he grew ever larger. His eyes glinted when he faced Ts'ai-Ho.

"Humans don't even know we're here, and if they did, these thick-skinned bastards wouldn't miss a step," Doren said.

Ts'ai-Ho tried to lighten the mood: "And you love them for it."

A smirk died on Doren's lips.

"I'm serious, Ts'ai. We're lost here."

"Perhaps you mistake your problem with that of all fairies," she said.

"I'm speaking on the plight of a people. Not some personal bullshit. Faerie will cease to be if we keep walking this path. We'll be fuppies with no soul. We'll start thinking remote controls are magic. That curses are just cuss words!"

Doren towered over Ts'ai-Ho now. She stood, raised her chin to meet his gaze, and spoke.

"Ah, I see. You don't want to be happy. You want to complain."

Doren blazed at her, his face turned a sepia tone that reminded Ts'ai-Ho of old temple photographs. Too late, she opened her mouth to speak softer words. Doren didn't give her the chance. He turned and ducked through the doorway, taking with him his dreaming eyes and handsome face, his open friendship.

After their argument Doren only showed his glamour, coming to her in guise. Yet Ts'ai-Ho had enjoyed the blue fireflies gathered at her bedroom windows. She had smiled at the homeless men holding primroses with her name etched into the petals. Because she believed that Doren would forgive her, and once more show his true face.

Ts'ai-Ho turns to the window on the far wall, hoping to glimpse a blue firefly. There's only a dark patch of sky and the fire escape zigzagging down the building next door. She stands looking at the mound of discarded bottles, diapers, and trash at the bottom of the escape.

Glamour.

The worry babies vibrate on top of the chest. Lan Ts'ai-Ho sweeps past and toward the front door.

The moon keeps its distance, shining down on Sugar Hill from just east of the Harlem River. Ts'ai-Ho stands in the grass outside of La Jupía's lair waiting to be invited in. Tsai-Ho does not sit on the wooden bench just behind her or lean against the low, black fence in front. She stays alert, holding her flute case firmly in her left hand.

La Jupía's permission wafts up from beyond the fence, a strong smell of oranges left too long in the sun. Ts'ai-Ho walks farther into the grass, stops just before the back end of Sugar Hill drops off into the dark.

La Jupía is there, little more than a shimmering, a Dominicana mirage that has been uprooted from the island and now patrols the caverns between tenement buildings from 139th to 155th. If anyone on the hill has seen Doren, La Jupía has.

Ts'ai-Ho removes her flute from the case and places it against her mouth, fingers poised. La Jupía comes closer. Her colors cluster; she is almost a form. Ts'ai-Ho plays her urgent question, a series of triplets that end with high notes. The question flutters near La Jupía. La Jupía meets the bit of spirit that Ts'ai-Ho and the flute have created, wraps herself around it. When her answer is ready, La Jupía pushes the song back into the flute. It has no more flavor than water: *No Doren, not today, not yesterday.*

Ts'ai-Ho plays another melody. It asks about the glamour Doren might be hiding behind. When La Jupía pushes the answer back into the flute, Ts'ai-Ho's throat burns with the spice of cayenne. *Glamour? I see spirit. I see all.*

~

As Ts'ai-Ho leaves La Jupía's lair and rounds the corner back to St. Nicholas Place, the lights of Yankee Stadium burn bright behind her. But there are other reasons that she looks shadowed and small. Ts'ai-Ho can't think of anyone else who might know Doren's whereabouts. She passes a pocket of people in front of her apartment building and stops at the phone booth near the fire escape. Ts'ai-Ho picks up the receiver and dials her home number. There are no new voicemails. She cues up Doren's message from this afternoon. When he starts speaking, she shuts out the street noise and focuses, trying to pick up clues from background noise. Her mind runs reels of Doren's demise while she listens: blood splattered across his fingers as he calls to say it's too late; the thump of his lifeless head lolling in her arms; the weak howl of anguish as Doren dissipates into the ether. She pushes away the images and plays the message again.

"My Ts'ai, it's done. I'm through, sick of—"

The worry babies drop into a shaft of moonlight at the bottom of the fire escape. In the second before each one passes from the light back into the dark, Ts'ai-Ho almost convinces herself that she has seen floating candy wrappers or some other mundane sidewalk flotsam. But standing single-file, close to the building, the worry babies are unmistakably extraordinary. There are half a dozen of them: red, blue, green, yellow.

They are so small Ts'ai-Ho can only see their color. The worry babies walk close to the building, just above the pavement, their magic hidden in the shadows where the brick meets concrete. When she recognizes them, Ts'ai-Ho stops listening to Doren's message and curses under her breath. She glances at her neighbors. Their conversations continue, uninterrupted.

Ts'ai-Ho places the receiver back in the cradle, following the worry babies with her gaze. They have hardly covered the distance of one of her strides. So, for now, she stands and marvels. Up to this moment, Ts'ai-Ho hasn't seen any hint of fairy magic in the worry babies, but now she is faced with a band of beings that bear little resemblance to the curios she thought she knew.

They head southeast, toward 155th street. As Ts'ai-Ho watches, they cross against the light and inch up the street's sharp incline. The C train station is at the top. As the worry babies go down the first stair, they drop out of sight. Ts'ai-Ho follows.

There are safer stations in the MTA than 155th Street. But few can compare with its entertainments: as Ts'ai-Ho descends onto the platform, a homeless man dressed in tatters shits a yellow load of last night and grunts to himself about the lack of privacy in subway stations. Ts'ai-Ho looks past him, searching the shadows.

The worry babies stand out among the dark spots of old gum on the ground. Ts'ai-Ho falls in behind them. A hot wind blows, signaling the arrival of the uptown train. Across the tracks, people trickle down in ones and twos, deserting the late-night benches to catch the train. Ts'ai-Ho follows the worry babies. She wonders what kind of fairy dust Doren spun into their thread to carry so much magic: life, invisibility ... teleportation.

Ts'ai-Ho feels the change before she sees it. Just as the train doors open for passengers on the other side of the station, an envelope of bottomless space appears in front of the worry babies. They step in. Before they can disappear, Lan Ts'ai-Ho is next to them, being sucked into a tight blackness that spits her out on the other side.

When she opens her eyes, the homeless man is above her, looking down. He wears a dark suit.

"You all right?" he asks.

He helps Ts'ai-Ho to her feet. As he does, concentric circles of lightheadedness radiate from the crown of her skull. Ts'ai-Ho realizes she hasn't eaten all night. Thoughts of food absorb the next few seconds. At the same time, the circles of Ts'ai-Ho's lightheadedness grow larger, and the right half of each crashes into the wall beside her. Ts'ai-Ho stares off into the distance and pictures dim sum delights.

The homeless man removes a handkerchief from beneath his suit and brushes off the knees of her slacks. The semi-circles reach the beams that separate the local and express tracks. There, they break apart and ripple into oblivion. As they shatter, Ts'ai-Ho notices them for the first time.

Before she can investigate further, she must get rid of the homeless man, lest he be alarmed by the seams of the city. Ts'ai-Ho turns to him.

He holds a corner of the handkerchief in each hand, trying to snap the dirt out of it. His suit is shiny black. The suit does not move as he snaps the cloth in the air. When his arms move, the arms of the suit lag behind and Ts'ai-Ho can see brown sleeves moving where the black suit does not. Peering closer, she can see an entire set of ragged, mismatched clothes beneath the suit. A strange veil of light glows between the two.

She decides that the homeless man doesn't need her protection.

"You sure you're okay?" he asks.

"Yes, thank you," she answers.

Ts'ai-Ho walks the length of the platform, checking the shadows for worry babies. The envelope of space still hangs in the air, a bit of not nothing that looks wetter than the air around it. But no worry babies. She walks back up to the street.

At first, Ts'ai Ho doesn't suspect the nature of the world she's crossed into. She stands on the corner of

155th and Amsterdam, looking for the worry babies in swatches of light on the sidewalk. A woman with curly dark hair and a burgundy messenger bag passes her, stepping off the curb. She only walks a few steps before a massive SUV squeals around the corner and stops within inches of hitting her. Its headlights spill onto her face. Burned rubber prickles in the back of Ts'ai-Ho's throat. After one tight breath the young woman looks up at the driver and looses a burst of expletives, her fingers grasping the small silver cross on her chest. When the "motherfucker"reaches the driver, his windshield explodes.

This is a first for Lan Ts'ai-Ho. In all her travels, from Penglai to Harlem and beyond, she has never been in a place where feelings have as much power as the ones who produce them. She immediately feels uncomfortable here and regrets it before she can stop herself. The regret beads up on her skin and slides down her arms. When it falls from her fingertips, regret crystallizes into a discomfort that pings against the sidewalk where it breaks.

The driver mistakes the sound for more of his own breaking glass. He starts to yell, and in his blind rage, his own curses shatter the other windows. The young woman walks away, snickering. Ts'ai-Ho breathes deeply and avoids eye contact. She worries what will happen if she connects with his emotions.

Before she can call her worry back, the worry babies stand in a circle, facing her. They are as tall as the street lamps. This large, their faces are terrible. The simple lines and circles of mouth and eyes are now a swarm of dark dots bleeding into each other.

The one closest to Ts'ai-Ho teeters on spindly thread-covered legs. Its large rectangular head sits forward from the rest of its body. Behind it the other five worry babies sway on equally thin green and blue legs. Their arms stick straight out from their bodies.

Ts'ai-Ho clears her throat. "Did you find Doren?" she asks.

The closest one steps closer; the others hang back. The leader then. It has no mouth to open and so stares intently at Ts'ai-Ho. She tries to think of a way to communicate, remembers the flute. She opens the case and brings the instrument to her lips. Before Ts'ai-Ho can play the first note, the lead worry baby bends down, its sideshow body bowing, and chomps down on the other end of the flute. Ts'ai-Ho's flute, her gateway to immortality and thousand-year friend, is lost in the dark maw of the creature's mouth. The worry baby steps back, closing the circle.

Ts'ai-Ho's shock knocks the wind out of her. As she tries to catch her breath, the worry babies vanish.

Ts'ai-Ho thinks that frustration will cascade from the sky and strike her down. It does not. Frustration, an electrical current, rivets her to the ground. It buzzes through her body, pauses in her teeth, then jumps into the nearest street lamp, and blows it out in a shower of orange sparks. Helplessness scurries in shortly after and crawls up Ts'ai-Ho's back. It scratches, lightly, maddeningly at her scalp until she runs back to the subway station. She heads straight for the spot of not nothing that brought her here and doesn't stop running until she spills out the other side.

Sunday morning is bright, bleaching the ceiling a shade of white that makes Ts'ai-Ho close her eyes before she rolls over and raises on her elbows to look at the answering machine that blinks ... blinks ... blinks.

At the northernmost tip of Manhattan, a piece of the ancient remains. Lan Ts'ai-Ho sits in Inwood Hill Park, the last 200 acres of primordial forest on the whole island, waiting for Doren. The morning air is fresh; the neighborhood sounds of Inwood distant. Ts'ai-Ho sits on a bench with her legs crossed loosely as a light wind blows the stray hairs on the back of her neck. On the message, Doren said he would meet her near the caves. She glances in the direction of their dark doors and wonders if he will leave her waiting for naught. Squirrels scuttle across the grass and climb up a gnarled maple; a painted lady butterfly stumbles through the air, comes close to Tsai-Ho's face, lands on the corner of the bench and stays there. A park ranger passes by, clipboard in one hand, bottled water in the other. When he leaves, Ts'ai-Ho is alone with her thoughts and the butterfly. She turns to it and speaks.

"You're well then?" she asks.

"Aye, I'm straight," it answers.

"Doren, could you—"

The butterfly's body bubbles out and joins together at the edges until it's a quivering brown sphere. It pops, raining a fine dust over Doren who now sits naked next to Ts'ai-Ho's shoulder, his mouth as high as her ear. Ts'ai-Ho blushes, moves her gaze to the empty spot just in front of Doren.

"I thought you had or were going to—"

He looks over, and his gaze stops the words. There is no glamour there, only a steadiness that makes Ts'ai-Ho wonder at its origin.

"I was worried," Ts'ai-Ho finishes.

"Trust." Doren's eyes brighten, and he smiles. "I know. Came close enough, truth be told."

A knot forms in Ts'ai-Ho's throat.

"Doren—" she begins.

"But it was reminded to me, by some very rude little dolls I might mention, that I've got some unfinished business—a new flute that needs carving, a thread that needs mending."

"It was only frayed, Doren," Ts'ai-Ho says. "What binds us can't be broken—like old world to new."

How the Carters Got Their Name

A lot of Black folks are walking around with their owner's last name. Or rather their ancestor's owner. Others are a little luckier. They're Johnson from Son of John. Baker 'cause that's what they did. Cobbler from the skill it took to earn that name. Ezekiel was one of these last. Sometimes he wished he were a son of John, though—'cause the Carters had earned their name in death and revolution.

His grandmother only told Ezekiel the story once. He had just finished weeding their garden and stood in the kitchen, gulping down sweet iced tea. Outside, it had been hot like it only got in the moist river valley of Kentucky: hot enough to take notice, but not to impose too much on the beautiful day. Grandma Maddie called him into the living room. She sat in her overstuffed armchair, watching one of the reparations protests with the sound turned off. A throng of brown faces filled the small screen, mouthing the same words. Their expressions said more than the placards they held, articulated their position better than a thousand raised fists. Grandma Maddie looked up from the scene and told Ezekiel to sit so she could tend to the rose bush scratches riddled down his arms. He settled at the foot of her chair, his shoulder resting against her knee. With both of Ezekiel's parents long ago passed away—his mother, into the grave, and his father, into the night—Ezekiel and Grandma Maddie shared the small confines of their country home with an uncommon grace.

Grandma Maddie plucked a fat leaf from the plant that stood on the chest near her chair. Above it, a blurry black and white daguerreotype of her great-grandmother hung. Only their expressions differed. Ezekiel's grandmother had deep laugh lines and a ready smile. The woman above looked as if someone had carved worry and hard work into her brow with a sharp stick.

Grandma Maddie broke open the aloe leaf. As she slid her finger through its milk, Ezekiel laid his arm across her lap and began to relax into the folds of her skirt.

"You did some good work out there today, Zeke," she said. "Should be able to get those cabbages into the space you cleared. Maybe some squash and more room for some yellow tomatoes." She said this to watch Ezekiel's face screw up in disgust, knowing how much he hated tomatoes, yellow or otherwise. Even in these food-lean times, when gardens were a necessity and livestock a luxury, he would rather go quietly hungry than eat them. She never tired of the joke, and unlike most twelve-year-old boys, neither did he.

Ezekiel had never been like his peers. His genius made him different. Though applying to biology programs left little time to spend with other kids, he doubted they would want to be with him anyway; his daddy didn't. Even with his stratospheric IQ, Ezekiel didn't believe that women or prison or selfishness had kept his father from him—though his Grandma Maddie, the man's own mama, had told him as much.

Because of his father's absence, or perhaps in spite of it, Ezekiel made it his business to know everything there was to know about being a Carter. He had almost exhausted what Grandma Maddie thought it proper to tell him. The Carters, it seemed, had been a raucous bunch right up to his grandmother—though really, it had been her "dealings with women" that earned her the title. She loved to put it that way, heavy on the sarcasm. The Carters, she said, lived loud because they knew that they would die young.

They didn't die from bullets or barroom brawls or overdoses either. Their bodies just turned on 'em one day, made them suffer like hell for a spell, and then gave up with the soul inside screaming. That's the way Grandma Maddie always put it. She had a way of putting things. On this particular day his grandmother decided to acknowledge his burgeoning manhood by way of telling Ezekiel how the Carters got their name.

"Zeke, today I'm gonna tell you something special." She dabbed the aloe under his eye where a deep groove of blood had sprouted. "Boy, how'd you do that? Looks like it hurts like bajeezus." Looking into his eyes, she said, "You gotta be more careful with yourself." She stroked the soft dense hair on his head. Ezekiel moved closer, breathed deeper.

"It ain't a pretty story, but it's the truth." She paused, collecting another swipe of aloe from the reserve on the back of her hand.

"A lot of Black folks are walking 'round with their owner's last name. Or rather their ancestor's owner. Others are a little luckier. They're 'Johnson' from 'Son of John'. 'Baker' 'cause that's what they did. 'Cobbler' from the skill it took to earn that name. The Carters are like that.

"Way back before you or even I can remember, we was slaves. Not like the processing pools in Brandermill or even the way them reparations people talk about it, but real slaves. Hanging tobacco, sweating in the fields, hearts long broke. There are stories for every one of them days, but this is about the day before the day we got our name.

"The way it was told to me, a young girl had been taken in the night by the overseers. In front of her mama. Which, unfortunately, was nothing new. But on that day something in the mama snapped—like a stepped-on stick that whips up at the one who broke it. She started screaming and jumped on them overseers. Went straight for the eyes, as it was told to me. She broke noses when they tried to restrain her, shattered teeth, closed windpipes with her bare feet, kicking out against all those restraining arms and hands. Four men couldn't stop her fury, the protecting of her child. Outside the cabin the people had started to gather. As it was told to me, their eyes filled the small window and doorway of the cabin. They watched as the mama blinded two of the men, and was working on a third when the head man, himself, came barreling through the doorway and shot her right there—back of the head, like a coward would. Blasted her all over the cabin and the screaming child. By the time the echo cleared, all hell had broken loose.

"The people had caught a fury. Any other day, they might have dragged themselves away. In the morning they would have cried for the woman slung up on a tree, split from hind to head. But not on that day. There was no reason other than their lives."

Ezekiel's eyes nearly vibrated in their fullness. He didn't realize that he gripped his Grandma Maddie's thigh like the last solid thing on an endless sea.

"They ran, not to the paths that led through the woods, but straight toward the bright house on the hill. Some were shot down before they'd even gone a few steps, picked off by the head man. Their arms reached out even in death, trying to grab some of the vengeance surging toward that house. They lit fires in the field as they went, moving as one. The people had no plan, no weapons. They carried only the weight of their years. And with that, they tore the place apart."

In his mind's eye Ezekiel could see the people moving—splintering wood and tearing down doors. His gaze drifted to the television set, settled on the tumult that filled the screen. The two images merged—all these people fighting for something when there was so little left. The force of their union pulled him away from his grandmother and further into the world. He sat next to her, his back now so rigid and straight it seemed as if his shoulders were pulled from above.

"Soon enough, the head man found more men and more guns. When the shooting and screaming were done, and the birds came back to the trees to soothe the earth that had witnessed it, there were more bodies than people. The folks who had survived were beaten, strung up. Our ancestor, Brother, was one of the first to be put back to work, hefting and carrying the bodies of man, woman, and child. He placed them softly as he could into a waiting wagon. He was so good at the task, so swift and so strong, that they made it his job." Grandma Maddie shifted in her chair and tilted her head with a sad smile. "Brother worked the death cart until he was the one laid."

Tiny scratches forgotten, Ezekiel wrapped his arms around his knees, head cradled between them. He gazed into a distance that he now knew he would someday meet. Grandma Maddie placed her hand on his shoulder.

"... And that, Ezekiel, is how the Carters got their name."

Deep Night

Between death and birth lies a deep night. In it, the soul stretches out, comes apart at the seams, and disperses, to eventually recreate itself anew. Evangeline always imagined it to look like multicolored light floating like gossamer or lightning in space. She thought now of her Mama Luella stretched out against the darkness, melding with other lights while Evangeline sat stiff-backed and tired in a clearing to pay her respects. She smiled through the distance between them now. She did not fear that Mama Luella was lost, only traveling to come back in another face, a deeper dream, a more refined version of her truth. Evangeline looked now and again at her father sitting next to her. Only the tendons in his jaw acknowledged the funeral happening around him; they worked diligently, chewing on the pain of death. His round brown face was still but for their movement. The rest of him seemed far away. She hoped with her mother.

Activity coursed around them. Graceful old mamas crowned in feathered Sunday hats led each other to their seats, spoke and wept quietly in pockets of color—blue, purple, rose. All of Mama Luella's favorite colors expressed in skirts, homemade blouses, dyed slippers—as per her grandmother's instructions. Evangeline didn't wonder when they'd received these instructions. Only her father and the Reverend donned the traditional black. She wore the dress she'd found waiting for her in her grandmother's front bedroom, a lush blue wrap with white doves stitched into the hem. Though she'd never worn a wrap in her life, her hands worked outside her conscious mind and cinched it perfectly in a few moments, a deep hum vibrating through her lips as the last fold was tucked in place.

Evangeline smiled now at the women she knew had bathed her grandmother at this morning's sunrise. Carefully dipping swatches of cloth ripped from their own lives into spring water, they had wiped off the funeral parlor's makeup and concealer, coaxing Luella out of this impression of her. Now they turned the corners of their mouths up, smiling back at Evangeline. They slowly nodded to her, eyes locked on her own. She returned the gesture. It seemed a signal.

The Reverend, who'd been quietly praying in a cluster of oaks, advanced from the trees and walked to the front of the outdoor congregation. He smoothed his thick white mustache and began to collect the spirit.

"Brothers and sisters, we gather today to celebrate the soul of Luella Willet ..."

"Mmmm hmmm," the mourners sang back to the Reverend.

"... Sister Luella touched all of our lives, but more than that, she touched the heart of God!"

"*Yes*, she did! Yes, she *did*!" the older ladies chimed in, fanning the words out of their mouths. Evangeline watched them scoot farther back in their chairs, poised for the next punctuation.

"... and for this we *know* she sits *high* in the kingdom of the Lord!"

"On *high*! Yes, Lord on *high*!" came the crescendo from the audience.

Having released this energy built up since they learned of her passing, Luella's longtime friends and distant acquaintances settled back in their seats to let the familiar funereal words unfold. Evangeline sat quietly, open, absorbing the Tuscaloosa that had been lost to her since her mother forbade her to visit.

~

"Where do you come from?"

"Long time 'go, the way-back folks come from there to here to learn how to be reborn right here on the land. With the trees and all the little animals and everything and they stay alive so there'd come us, and here us is." The gravel slid from Evangeline's throat. She said in her own voice, "Here us is." Evangeline rocked slightly, small hands cupping the wet bark of the log. As her "is" flowed out across the water, Evangeline looked up to catch Tasha's naked expression. She'd learned to look before Tasha covered up the tense eyebrow, the pinched corners of her mouth. This time her friend's face was open, the lips parted slightly. Tasha looked ready to ask another question but then nodded to herself, dismissing it. Behind her the water continued to push through the earth, clear water over pastel pebbles. Evangeline and Tasha fell now into one of their silences, the end of a game they played throughout the few weeks Evangeline spent in Tuscaloosa visiting her Mama Luella.

Nearly every day Tasha and Evangeline would strike out just after lunch and spend whole afternoons lost in the half acre behind the shed. They were a good pair: Tasha had many questions and Evangeline, answers. Twenty Questions was their favorite game. Though it always had the same theme, they never tired of playing it. No one was better at "Who Am I?" than Evangeline. They'd walk through the woods, Tasha swatting at dandelions and weeds with her ever-present stick, bringing up the rear to Evangeline's searching eyes. When Evangeline had found something—a little waterfall emptying into a sinkhole, a leaf turned transparent by the sun, a rock whose texture tickled her—she'd hold it, if only with her eyes. Her face would smooth, and then Tasha knew Evangeline was ready.

Tasha would start with simple questions but had learned not to ask for the name because the answer was always "Evangeline." Never mind that two questions before she'd said she was six feet tall or in answer to the one before that that she made boats for a living. This was the trick in their game: that the answer was never one word or two, but the answers to all the questions stacked up together. It wasn't the "I" that was important but the "am." Tasha found this more interesting than television and spent most of her time with Evangeline. Tasha didn't assume that she knew things so she wasn't afraid to ask questions; that's what Evangeline liked about her. Most people thought they knew every damn thing. When really what they knew wasn't any deeper than the stream behind her grandmother's house.

"How come your Mama don't like Black people?" Tasha asked into the silence.

Evangeline slid down the log and onto the ground, tucking her long legs beneath her. "Why do you think that?"

"'Cause she don't. You can tell. It's like she don't want to touch us or something. Too good for her own kind, my Mama say."

Wondering if it were true, Evangeline said, "That's not true," and picked up the end of Tasha's stick, dragged it lightly across the grass. Evangeline knew what her friend was talking about but didn't think that was what her mother added up to.

Just before Evangeline had come to Tuscaloosa—she loved saying that word, fast and happy. It sounded like a secret password, *Tuscaloosa*—Marie told Evangeline that her legacy was to struggle and blossom. Evangeline told her mother that she wasn't delicate enough to blossom, that she'd rather explode like popcorn: "*Uh*! Here I is!" Marie said all girls were delicate and pointed at the soft blonde woman on the TV screen. After that, Evangeline thinned herself out, cut back her thoughts, stopped eating butter. Marie told Evangeline that they were beyond color, and if White isn't a color, they were. 'Cause most times white was the only color Van saw: at school, Brownie meetings, play dates. She went to a private school in a private neighborhood. To Evangeline private meant White. Except for her private dreams. Not wanting to play Twenty Questions again, Evangeline shut down that train of thought and looked up at the lavender sky.

"Come on, it'll be dark soon." The girls brushed off their backsides and headed to the shed for jars. Their favorite blue lightning bugs came out earliest of all.

That evening, Tasha's parents, the neighbor's family, and Evangeline's got together for a barbeque. Marie and Edward had gotten in earlier that evening to spend the traditional last weekend with Mama Luella. Now they sat outside talking with the other adults. Mama Luella stood over a barrel grill spraying water onto the meat. In the family room Tasha and Evangeline played with Marcus, the neighbor's boy.

"You ain't all *that*! You ain't all *that*!" Marcus yelled, his chin pointing upward on the last syllables as he looked down his nose at Tasha. The sound of his voice excited him at this volume. Before, Tasha had been winning the Dozens, cutting on his brother's too-big nylon jacket and the way it looked on his pointy tall boy body, even noticing that he'd tied his shoes in knots where the laces were broken. He'd lost the rhythm of the contest, could think of no comebacks and so was left listening to a list of his faults. But now Marcus had her—not with wit but with sheer size and volume. Tasha retreated closer to the wall every time he yelled. He liked the power, and bully genius stoked his voice. His hand flashed out, grabbed the doorknob behind her, and before she could make real words with her grunts of protest, he'd shoved her into the darkened closet. Immediately her voice reached its highest pitch, sirening for someone to get her out.

Of course, it was Evangeline who came to the rescue. Already well over four feet at seven years old, she was a natural protector. Used to plucking the smaller girl out of trouble, Evangeline enjoyed this role. This made her walk slowly over to Marcus, preparing her strategy. Before a word came out of her mouth or a hand up to protect herself, he'd grabbed her too and shoved her on top of Tasha, whose hysterics bounced off the walls in the small black space.

Evangeline knocked the wind out of her. The screaming cut off, lost in the gush of Tasha's breath. In the moment of silence when the other senses faded, Evangeline's skin took over and told her that the warm sweat pressed against her was too close, that the hot breath on her neck was fear. Then it failed her. It could not tell her that this was not the dream where a box of darkness fell on her as she walked in another life, through the abundant plains. The one that blotted out the blue skies and breeze, sealing her away from that happiness. Evangeline reacted now as she did then, the last time something tried to take the space out of her soul. When her hands spread out and hit the closet's walls, it began: the timbre that got straight to the core of things, a sound beyond sound.

Marcus snapped to attention, his grin breaking apart until the boy looked like he'd been struck in the face. The tendons stood out on his neck. His head vibrated from tension. He looked about to cry.

Conversation on the back porch stopped short. Tasha's and Evangeline's mothers wavered in the wind. While Tasha's screams dissipated into the sounds of Earth, Wind and Fire, Evangeline's cut straight through, reaching through the women. Only their eyes shifted—gravitated, in fact—toward the sound. The men sitting out under the magnolia tree looked at their wives for an explanation. Cans of beer hovered in midair. Startling stretched into taut awe.

Mama Luella moved. Evangeline's screaming frightened her, almost made her panic. The sound was too raw and thick for a child's delicate cords. She tore the door open and went to pick up the girl. Her eyes stopped the big woman.

Mama Luella thought she saw something in them, moving across the whites. Mama Luella shook her head hard once and took Evangeline in her arms. The sound didn't stop until Mama Luella pulled Evangeline clear of the closet. In the light the child's eyes cleared. Evangeline stared out into the distance, pupils straight ahead and expanding. Her parents' running feet shook the floorboards. Evangeline hopped a little in the air but stood still, rooted to the spot. She didn't speak another word all through dinner, only nodding when asked if she were okay. The adults spoke quietly, moved sharply, knocked over a salt shaker and a pitcher of iced tea, sliced through a wishbone. Her father, usually out playing bid whist or pool with the neighborhood men, watched TV all night and stuck close to his daughter.

Evangeline spoke only after the visitors had gone and the dinner plates were put away. In the front bedroom Marie folded Evangeline's clothes back into a tiny pink suitcase as Mama Luella laid the child down for rest.

"Mama Luella, what dreams mean?" Evangeline asked.

"Dreams are your soul remembering what's been done and what's to come."

"Mother! I will not have you filling her head with all that foolishness," Marie interrupted. "Haven't we had enough for one day?" She turned toward her daughter. "Dreams are like storybooks, Evangeline. You're just telling stories to yourself."

Marie looked steadily into the child's eyes, trying to beam out authority. Evangeline looked at her a moment and then focused on her grandmother with wide eyes and closed mouth. Mama Luella only gazed calmly at the child, smoothing the tasseled blanket over Evangeline's feet, then turned, and walked out of the bedroom. Later Evangeline heard her mother and grandmother arguing in whispers out in the kitchen:

"Just 'cause you don't wanna know, don't mean the child don't."

"Gracious! And you wonder why I left Tuscaloosa. Too many backward people and their backward ideas."

"You can be as saditty as you want, Marie Mae, but don't sass me like you didn't come out me, ya hear."

"Now, Mama ..."

"Now, Mama," and then the screen door banging shut, feet following after.

That night Evangeline dreamed of her Mama Luella, shrunk down to her size with a little girl's face and strong hands. The Girl Mama Luella carried a bucket across a dusty patch of land, her gaze brushing the grass. Evangeline couldn't see all of her own dream self, only its hand—large, brown, and mottled with scars. She watched as it took the burden out of the other's small hands and grasped them. The Girl Mama Luella looked up and smiled. A beautiful brown girl who'd been waiting to smile. Its flash faded slowly from Evangeline's unconscious eye, first the color, then the presence.

The last remnants of floating light melded into the golden sun splashed across Evangeline's face when she awoke.

The next morning Evangeline repeated the action, taking her grandmother's hand after breakfast. Rubbing the child's supple knuckles, a tear slid down Mama Luella's cheek. She gathered the girl in her arms and placed her in her lap. "I just want you to be safe." Mama Luella kissed Evangeline's forehead, and she rested against her rock. Through morning's first shy rays toward the full beams of early afternoon, they sat that way, not moving until the car was packed and Ed came to say goodbye, collecting Evangeline. Marie sat in the front seat of the Volvo, reading a magazine. As the car pulled away, Evangeline smiled big for her Mama Luella.

When her mother read one of the child's letters to her grandmother the following autumn, Marie Brown decided she didn't like what came out of her daughter in the backwoods of her childhood, and Tuscaloosa became a memory to Evangeline.

But Evangeline remembered more than her mother could fathom. That much was evident even in the letter that changed everything. Marie had been cleaning Evangeline's room, looking for any loose ends that could be sent down to their new home in Savannah. Edward stood in the doorway again asking why they couldn't just wait and do everything at once when Evangeline was done with the school year. Marie turned and leveled her eyes upon him.

"Edward, the sooner we start, the sooner we finish."

"But we still have lives here, Marie, things that have to get done before the move. I've got two projects to finish at the firm. Van's got her million and one classes and clubs, and you—"

"And I am keeping this family in order, moving us on to new things. Don't you want to take the next step, Edward? Or do you want to stay at a mediocre firm where they don't appreciate you? Or maybe you want our daughter to have to grow up around this mess like we did?"

"What mess, Marie? I've been listening to you talk about 'this mess' for months. I don't see any mess, except for the one we're making trying to hurry this move."

"Oh, don't lose your reason now and don't take that tone with me. Don't you trust my judgment?"

"Of course I trust your judgment, Marie. That's not the point. It's just that these last couple of months, you've been ... agitated or something, I don't know."

"And this move is just what I need—what we all need. To settle down somewhere safe. That's all, Edward. The thought of it just ... excites me." She moved in close, put her arms around his neck and looked up into his nutty brown face, reassuring herself that yes, she had married the right man for the job. "Nothing to worry about. Soon there won't be anything to worry about." She kissed him, letting just enough warmth out to calm his fears. "Savannah's going to be great, hon. We're going to be great in Savannah."

Edward looked down and saw his Marie, bit the side of his mouth, and nodded. He held her for a moment, brought her close to him, and then backed away.

"I have to get back to work," he said and turned down the hallway.

She watched him round the corner and then returned to her work. Packing away some of Evangeline's books, Marie came across the letter sticking out of an old National Geographic. She unfolded and read:

> *Mama Lu. How are you? I miss you. Did you eat all the tomatoes in the garden? Will you send me some? Mama never buys them. She cooks little green pencils. They tast like yuck. We are moving soon. Their will be a grate school. I can take better clases. Mama say she sick of the fokes here. Say they a bad enflunce. I had a dream with the hurt lady. I have a lot. She still says no thing. She looks at me. She smiles and tuches my face. I know she will say sum thing soon. I want her to talk. Are dreams what you say or what Mama say? The hurt lady is not like a dream. I play kick ball and go to the beech when I dream. Not like when I see her. I love you.*
>
> *Love*
> *Evangeline*

This was the last letter never sent from Evangeline to Mama Luella. When they moved to Savannah, Marie redoubled her efforts to fill up her daughter's mind with activities and near constant instruction on how to act. Marie spent every waking moment standing over Evangeline, whether she was physically there or not. At night Marie took two prescriptions so she could do it all again in the morning. She meant to make Evangeline cultured by her definition, to follow in her footsteps and beyond—but most of all, she meant to leave no room for the hurt ladies in Evangeline's dreams. The girl was a fledgling ballerina by eight, a Girl Scout with every badge by eleven, and a formidable chess opponent by thirteen. Amongst her mother's perfumed and perfectly coiffed crowd of pale friends there was talk of geniushood. Through the martini glasses clinking in the parlor, the subtle tones of jealousy could be heard between the congratulatory words, the exclamations of great mothering. Marie accepted these compliments with a chiseled smile. Her gaze stayed cast in front of her, darting toward the clock on the mantle, counting the minutes until it was time to shuttle Evangeline from French tutoring to gymnastics.

Mama Luella wrote over the years, first demanding, then begging that she be allowed to see her grandchild. She called Marie out for severing the connection and trying to hide her own dreams. Mama Luella told Marie that no good would come of it—and she was right. *It won't stop just because you want it to, Marie. You can't run from it. You should be running* to *it.*

Marie scoffed at this last, but it came back to her many times over the years: as she sat in PTA meetings, a little brown dot in a sea of white; once as she watched the waves rippling up the shore on a vacation to Virginia Beach with Edward's friends; that time the butcher mistook her for Evangeline and called her "girl"; every night, as the chalk of the little blue pills melted onto her tongue, Marie thought of her mother's words blurring on the page she still kept in her nightstand drawer. When it came time for Evangeline to graduate high school, Marie wrote her mother back. *Mama, please come*. The pills weren't working.

There were signs, of course, but like most, her family didn't see them until after: little things could be found out of place in the fastidiously clean bedroom that she and Edward shared. Twice, when she was supposed to pick her daughter up, she found herself out by a lake staring deep into the water, looking at it as if there were no bottom at all. Marie started to avoid her friends. Their crumbling pale faces vaguely nauseated her. She found herself staring at the way this one's mouth was drooping into a tight frown or that one's chin expanded, grew ruddy and flaccid connecting to the neck. They looked alien to her, these proper White women she'd spent formal brunches and dinners with. Marie could no longer stand to be around those who had once been so valuable to her and, more importantly her daughter's, opportunities. She declined invitations to galas and golf tournaments. After the incident at a dinner party hosted by Edward's company, Marie could no longer control the remembering, and it came back to her in a whirlwind.

Edward was off mingling with clients, buttering up his boss for a promotion. She could hear his clear baritone ringing out among the other voices. The glass of champagne in her hand kept Marie connected to the room. She concentrated on its cold mingling with her skin. She didn't see the man approach her from behind.

"Mrs. Brown." His voice slithered. She turned abruptly to find Matthew Leonard, one of Edward's associates—by far her least favorite—standing before her in a crowded, brown three-piece suit. A dim red rose stuck out of the lapel.

"How *lovely* to see you again." All the time he spoke his gaze moved up her body, lingering on the ample curves and muscles shrouded in the purple wrap.

"Mr. Leonard," Marie replied, giving only the most obligatory of responses.

"You're looking fabulous—but then again you always do." Not waiting for a reply, he continued, "Catherine and I are having a little affair next weekend. You know, just a little something in commemoration of the upcoming commencement, a bit of a celebration for the ones who've been paying those exorbitant private school fees all these years." He laughed at his own joke. "We were really hoping you and

Edward could stop by. After all, Evangeline is the valedictorian, and the four of us should have been coupling up a long time ago. "

Marie looked at him sharply at this last comment. Immediately, she knew it was a mistake to look him in the eye. His face was poised in a lascivious sneer.

"I'll really have to ask Edward about that," she replied, looking over his head for her husband. She'd lost his laughter in the crowd. "Evangeline's speech at the NAACP awards ceremony is that night. We've already made quite a few commitments."

"Not too many, I hope. They have a way of dictating our lives, don't they?" he said, and took a step closer. "I, myself, try to stay open to the possibilities." As he spoke, his hand crossed the threshold of insinuation and rested on her hip. "Would you care to dance, Marie?" he asked, his hand moving toward her ass.

In one motion Marie moved close to his ear, broke her glass on the side of the table, brought it against his thigh, and whispered, "Would you care to bleed, Matthew?"

The sharded glass shook in her hand. Slowly Marie moved her head around his and looked him in the eye. He thought he saw something moving across the whites and took two quick steps away from her.

"Marie! I see we've had a little accident." Edward moved up briskly from the other side of the room. "Let me get someone." He called out to a waiter and then turned back to his wife.

For a moment Marie kept her back to him. Then she took a deep breath, making sure to look at the floor first and replied, "Yes, it seems so," handing him the broken glass. "I'm afraid I don't feel very well, Edward. Can we go?"

"Of course."

They left Leonard staring at the spot they'd been standing in.

~

That night dreams came back to Marie—through the veil of sedatives and the wall of her stalwart restraint. Marie's woman came back to her.

"Why you hidin'? You can't hide, girl! You can't hide!"

Marie could see the White face clearly in the blackness of the hold. She tried to breathe only when water lapped against the hull. She wanted to close her eyes and fade into the safe blackness, but she was afraid of not seeing the White man who searched her out, stepping on people, feces, and rats to find her. She scooted closer to the wall, balancing herself on the dead man beneath her. She tried not to recognize his marks, the same etched across her own face. The sleeping Marie knew this memory and didn't want it to see its end. She steeled herself against what was coming. Before his hand grabbed her, she blinked out and turned her inner eye to imagining the stars outside were familiar. He slapped her hard across the face, bringing her back. Her eyes reacted and opened. The White man was gone.

"Why you hiding?" the woman asked, her face floating warmly inches from Marie's. "You can't hide, child. We belong to each other. You can't deny me. Don't you see that?"

The next morning Marie wrote the message to her mother and began counting the days until Mama Luella's arrival. She threw away the pills when she got back from her morning errands. When Evangeline pulled into the driveway, she saw a sight: Marie digging up the side of the yard, planting yams in place of the stone garden she'd laid out piece by piece the previous spring. Marie came in while Evangeline was sitting at the table poring over a thick volume of Lacan.

"Why don't you stop straining your eyes and call your grandmother? Tell her about the NAACP ceremony," she said and walked out of the room. At first perplexed, Evangeline quickly recovered and picked up the phone.

Two days later Mama Luella was to arrive. The next day the neighbor's septic tank backed up and exploded all over his yard. The smell was horrific. Edward suggested that they stay at a hotel for a night or two.

"There's too much left to do. I don't want to celebrate Van's graduation in a hotel," Marie said. "Besides, Mama's coming, and I want her to be in our home. Not some strange bed in a strange place. We'll just close the windows, burn some potpourri. It can't last long. Remember, they're the ones without a toilet. I'm sure it'll be fixed soon."

And it was: two days after they took Marie away, as Edward and Evangeline climbed into a cab bound for the airport, workmen packed away their tools and prepared the broken valve for its final resting home at the Savannah City Dump.

One might say it was the smell that pushed Marie over the edge, or the possibility of finally talking to Mama Luella about the dreams, or maybe even the thought of letting Evangeline go off into the world. One might say this and be right, but this is what happened.

On May 22, 1999, the day before darling Evangeline's graduation, the Browns received one phone call and one package. The call came just before they were about to leave for the airport. Marie and Evangeline, focused on picking up Mama Luella, ignored the ringing. Edward picked up the receiver, expecting a call from work. He was on the phone for approximately thirty seconds. In that time his face flowed from easy expectation to stoic gravity. Afterwards, he sat his women down in their impatience and spoke the words he wanted to bottle up and save for another day.

"Mama Luella ..." he began. The story was simple: the rain, the cars, the crash. Its meaning was profound. Light turned to darkness, expectation turned to grief, joy to sorrow. Evangeline's day turned into Mama Luella's life. The house was silent; shadows hung in the room. Evangeline began to cry, first quietly then in long, ragged breaths. Edward tried to comfort her, smoothing the hair away from her face. He looked at his wife. She was not there. A woman made of stone stared back at him.

She stood up and walked out of the room. Edward heard her mount the stairs and close the bedroom door behind her.

Sometime later the doorbell rang ... and rang ... and rang. Finally, Edward answered it and the house returned to silence. It was a package with two names written on the front:

To: Evangeline Brown
From: Luella Price

He stood there trying to decide. In the end, he walked past his own closed bedroom door and into his daughter's room.

"It's from your Mama Lu," he whispered and left the package in Evangeline's trembling hands.

She didn't know what to do with it at first, that thing her grandmother had brought her even after she was gone. Evangeline opened it though and found her Mama Lu's love for her wrapped up tidy in Fed Ex cardboard. She read the letter first.

> *I write these words the night before my death. It was foretold to me in a dream. Do not grieve too harshly. Accidents don't happen at my age, Angel. You, my child, must prepare yourself. The time has come for sumthin that shoulda come a long time ago. But your mama wouldn't have it, nor your father. And livin in the white folks world has left you unprotected. I cannot leave this place with you so vulnerable, but by will alone I cannot stay. Do not be afraid, Angel. You cannot fear yourself, and that child is what's coming. You're catching up with*

yourself. Don't try to fit, just be. Not the Middle Passage, but a clear path. I can't tell you every detail 'cause I don't know. You children are made from different things than me and mine—our time, I mean. And you Angel are made up of something different altogether, I 'spect. Just try to remember you're becoming what you are.

Luella

Evangeline ran to tell her mother, finally to tell her mother about the woman in her dreams. She wanted to tell her all about herself, 'cause maybe Marie didn't know dreams weren't storybooks. The door was locked. Evangeline yelled for the first time in her house: "Mama! Mama, open the door! Mama, I want to see you! Mama! I want you to see me! Don't hide!"

Her voice cut through the darkness in the room. It cut through Marie's darkness. Marie could not respond. They were coming too fast on her—the colors and sounds from all her lost souls. But mostly from the first, from the one who traveled the waters.

Marie saw her mother, a young giant with wings enough to protect her from the waiting world. She saw the day that she closed the door between her selves, heard the reverberation of silence all over again. She saw her woman for the first time again: the strongest part of her spirit reaching out to touch her face when she was just a girl, five years old picking blueberries in Mr. Jackson's patch. She saw the splotches of blood on the tablecloth where she was born. The man in New Orleans who reached out to her then pale lemon hand: "Hey girl, you want a daddy?" The minstrel show that played out in the clearing. Choked on her first swig of whiskey that signaled her manhood in a remote village where green rolled strong and proud ever toward MacGillicuddy's Reeks. The little girl she'd seen cut in two by a train when the hulking monsters were still new to the world. Felt the heat of the brick oven the master's food simmered in. Tasted the sweat on her mother's breast when she came to her a few precious moments between sunset and rise. She even reached back and saw the water before the darkness that was her only ally when the hold doors closed, sealing the tomb of living bodies.

Marie tried to clear her mind, regain control. She took a deep breath, and the reek of human waste filled her nostrils. She closed her eyes, and there were the bodies. She started to hyperventilate. Each breath was another face. She reached out to grab hold of something and the curd of excrement was pasted across her hand. Marie could not hide. She reached her depth. Compelled by all that lay inside her, she began to remove her illusions.

Outside the door, time continued to slip into the past. Evangeline gave up her hoarse words at the door. Edward paced back and forth downstairs, eventually coming to rest on the other side of the bedroom door, his legs tucked under him, the right side of his body against the door. He slowly sang a song he thought he'd forgotten the words to, his cheek brushing the wood: "Marie ... Mae ... Marie ... Mae ... Marie, may I come in? Marie ... I ... Marie ... I ... Marie, I'll soothe your skin ... Marie ... Mae—"

The door to Evangeline's room swung open. Evangeline stood in the backlight bright as an angel; she wore a quilted robe of white. He recognized a piece of linen napkin at the hem. It was from his wedding.

"Mama Lu's graduation gift," she said, reaching down to help her father up. She pointed at the collar.

"From her favorite dress, the one she was baptized in ... and I think this pink piece is from Mama's birth. I don't know about the rest, but I will."

He kept staring at her face. It brought him peace.

"Daddy, I've got to go give this speech. I've got something to say. I want you to be there. Mama won't come out 'til she comes out," she added matter-of-factly.

Edward turned back toward the wood standing between him and his Marie, laid his palm flat against it.

"Daddy, I need you." The words were like magic. Edward stood up tall, brushed off his clothes, and walked down the stairs.

"Mama," she whispered, leaning into the door. "Don't be afraid. Bring them together. We'll be waiting for you, Mama."

Inside the dark room Marie stopped her scissors in mid-air and smiled. When she heard the front door close she continued to remove all the soul-less things from her. Later she moved on to the rest of the house.

While her mother stacked dishes, clothes, and furniture into a neat pile in the backyard, Evangeline walked up to a podium, exuding a confidence that flowed over the sea of brown faces stretched out before her.

"I had a speech prepared for tonight, but I won't be reading it. The world has changed since then. Today Luella Rivers Price died. She was my grandmother. But that's not why I'm telling you. She gave me a message, one so important that she could not go without passing it on to me. This is purpose and devotion. Tonight I operate in her honor, in the service of purpose and devotion, to deliver my own message. And that is simply this: integrate your spirits. We who are so wrapped up in the concept of integration in the schools, in the workforce, even in families. We who need it the most, not to better, but to survive whole, speak no words and make no effort to integrate our spirits. I'm here to tell you that you have more than one. I'm here to tell you that every voice inside you must be given a chance to speak. I'm here to tell you that there is no greater gift or accomplishment or reward than a soul that is strong, coherent, and free. Each one of you has been here before and will be again."

With this she walked off the stage and to her father. Edward put his arms around her, squeezed her closer to himself, and kissed her forehead. The two walked out of the darkened room, not hearing the applause or pausing between their strides. They took one step after another into the evening.

When they took Marie away she was a different woman. Her hair hacked off, nails broken off to jagged weapons. Blood trickled down her face. Her finery laid to waste in the bonfire only now cooling in the backyard. Walking between two men in white, she was dressed simply in a brown dress, with no shoes upon her feet. She hummed a low song to herself and intermittently spoke what the attendants thought was gibberish but was actually Wolof, one of her first languages. The others being English, French, Gaelic, and more Creoles than it makes sense to mention. One of the last things she did before getting into the back of the van was reach down, grab a handful of dirt, and put it in her pocket. Then Marie turned, pushed her palm high toward her family, and got in with the brown man idling the engine. For a moment the white and orange lights lit up the yard and then there was only darkness surrounding the two figures standing in the front lawn.

"You know what 'medium' mean, Mama? 'Medium' mean halfway through. That's you and me—mediums. You went too far one way, and I thought you were too far in another, but the woman come to me again last night. She said you be all right soon, she say you shouldn't have delayed it so long, that it'll leave its mark, but you be all right. And I'll be here with you, Mama ... my child's child. We'll walk back into the world together. Go anywhere you want. This is a hard thing, but I'm with you. Daddy'd like to see you ... well, when you're ready, if you want. Later, I dreamed you someplace beautiful, Mama. There were houses made out of wood and mud, painted yellow and red and white. Even the ground was painted beautiful. You sat outside next to a river staring into such blue waters. You were smiling. Then a woman called you, and you came running, so happy. I've never seen you smile like that. I hope you're there now. I hope you're there right now."

Marie's lips moved a bit and then were still again. Looking up at her daughter for the first time in months, she saw her eyes were clear and smiling.

Only Then Can I Sleep

I, Dainadella Adu, commit this to the skin of our ancestors, of which I am one, so that those who come after may know, and save their imagination for dreaming.

Six Days Before the Last

When I was a boy I did not believe the journals. I thought the transition would hurt. I imagined my spirit sucked out, like a night beetle by a hungry delau. When I was a girl I feared the molting, as I then feared anything that could not be stopped once begun. Now I know: it is simply the next breath. It took me seven transitions to understand that. But now I am at threshold, barely able to believe that my last transition, the one to my final body, approaches.

Janju laughs at my disbelief and keeps assuring me that it's true. After much searching, the Spirit Women found my match amongst the CanBal and have triggered my molt. After I have thresholded I will be promoted to a High Judge, an honor to any Djeli. So again, I'm writing here, in a now-careworn piece of hide torn by my first hand.

I am the only one to threshold in four seasons. When I began, hundreds transitioned into their last bodies, last lives. Not so, these nights. Some Djeli charge that the bodies are slowing us down, even stopping us from transitioning. They insist we shouldn't harvest them from wars. After problems with the last crop, a few brought their complaints to the courts. I have judged matters of trade and so have not been privy to the details. They are wrong, though. It is our honor that is infected, not the bodies we use. Fewer and fewer Djeli honor their trades. Instead they cite obscure statutes or quote a past life lesson to avoid a fair barter.

Until the transition I am left alone with my thoughts—and Janju's distractions. We intend to get all the use out of this host that we can. I have to stop calling it a host body. Soon I'll be in my body. What a strange phrase.

Five Days Before the Last

I shared the morning meal with this host body's new match, Uvonia. She seemed satisfied enough with it, although she remarked that the jaw cracks when chewing. Funny, I had forgotten. When I was new to it I cursed the noise every morning. Each time I yawned I feared it would fall right off the hinge. I had meant to get it fixed, but never did. At the time its more obvious tics—the flinching at loud noises or bright lights, and its food hoarding that passed for slow metabolism—took precedence. During the medical visits to fix those problems, I had overlooked the jaw.

Uvonia accompanied me to my check-up and, as a matter of course, consented to its condition. (I have known only one Djeli who would not consent: Radhuri Anatol, Case 44274 Cyle 23 in the Special Collections, and only as a performance in pursuit of her artist's guild membership. When the accolades faded, she quickly desisted and transitioned just before the molting would have left her forever afloat).

The next time I see Uvonia she will look as I have for the last twenty-eight years. She will smirk when she intends to smile, just I have. She will lead with her left foot and walk on her toes.

How these bodies hold on to their memories.

Not ~~the~~ my new body, though. It will only remember what I teach it to.

Four Days Before the Last

Janju has gone to check my body for me. I want her to describe it to me so I can see her face when she says the words. Otherwise I will never know if it pleases her. This body, though, is hungry and can't wait for the afternoon meal. Porren and plen with ripe shipi. It's this body's favorite new dish. It reminds me of the ackale and sweet tsitan fruit I ate as a youth. Not the same texture in it, though—nothing in it to rub your tongue against. Perhaps I will find something fresh-fresh later.

I hope Janju returns soon. So I can satisfy both my hungers.

Three Days Before the Last

I will write this slowly so that it bleeds.

My body ate Janju.

I found her host body, quiet and empty, next to the incube where my new body should have been. I thought to surprise her so that we could dine together at the city gardens or perhaps go dancing while we are still the same height. Instead I discovered her host body. Its features had already melted into a blank repose devoid of Janju's passion; the limbs lay still as stone. My body had picked her clean.

The Corps are searching for it with Janju trapped inside. They would not let me accompany them. I pray to Oddudua for Janju's safe return. When the time for judging ~~my~~ the body comes, I will pray for myself.

Two Days Before the Last

The Corps found my body sleeping next to Dunleve River. They tracked it by Janju's essence. They brought her—and it—here. Soon after, the Spirit Women arrived and laid the body out in the front room. I can hear them singing as they try to draw Janju out of the CanBal body and place her back in her host. The spicy smells of shreef and lacand fill the hallways. The body that had been matched to me has held her hostage for the better part of a day. Already she has fought bravely. Though our bond gives Janju an approximation, she and the body are not matched. Soon her own depleted host body will expire. Because I cannot help, I do not go where they lie. Instead, I walk around our home, touching Janju's things. I can still smell her spirit in the sheets, see it reflected in the sweet dark wine she always ~~drank~~ drinks before we sleep. They must get her out. They must.

One Day Before the Last

The trial begins this evening, in the open meadow near Gasca. Janju and I were bonded not far from there. When the Sanctified Judge wove our spirits together and presented us to the ancestor-stars, I knew I wanted to hold that position one day so that I could see Djeli love free and fresh-fresh with possibility. If only I had stayed on that judgeship level. Then I wouldn't have to decide our fates: mine, Janju's, Uvonia's. I cannot leave it to the Transgression Judge. Uvonia is only fit for this body, and I am only fit for the murderous one. Such a case is my jurisdiction.

Today, one of the Spirit Women told me what "CanBal" meant in the old tongue. If I could spare the strength, I would shake my head.

How these bodies hold on to their memories.

The Last Day

My molting period is almost over. I have made my decision. Let the ones who come after ponder it. I am too tired. I have done my judging.

Janju, forgive me. Oddudua, help me.

~

I, Janju Akanadella, commit this to the skin of our ancestors, of which I am one, so that those who come after may know, and save their imagination for dreaming.

The First Day

Air searches for a body to move in order to prove that it exists, even to itself; my Dainadella is this way. She ripples the wine in my glass so that I know she's here. Only then can I sleep.

Live Forevers

Even war couldn't take away the dew. The early morning sun glinted through the haze and lit up the scattered fields as the Woods' drove slowly through what was left of Erlanger, Kentucky. Jesse and William shared the backseat, while Raynard rode shotgun with Mama. The boys stared through the window, pointing at the scintillating grass, seeming just boys for a moment. Mama stole looks at Raynard and into the rearview mirror at her other two sons. She almost held her breath, not wanting to break the moment.

There was no dew left in Mound Bayou, just dirty smears of sooty condensation. Mississippi hadn't been a particularly pretty place since the Riders came back: broken windows, charred remnants of fool's crosses, misspelled hatred spewed on sidewalks and once-stately trees. But after the Klan Riders started burning the outposts and little towns that surrounded Mound Bayou, Thelma couldn't sweep the soot quickly enough to keep the porch from looking like a split coffin, freshly unearthed. She didn't want to sweep; out in the open air she could feel her neighbors' eyes piercing through her and into her home. She could feel those eyes searching past her, looking for her boys. They smiled all right—Miss Eunice, Brother Jerry, and the rest. They gave Thelma tight smiles that said "You best to enjoy it; time's almost up."

Before Thelma gave her precious triplets to the town that had helped pay their way, she brought them here, to the place that had created them just as surely as she had: Dr. Ezekiel Carter's hometown. Though Thelma knew Dr.

Carter was long laid in the ground, she also knew a place could make a person; just as surely as Mound Bayou had made her and her boys, yes indeed. Things being as they were, Thelma almost couldn't blame her community. But today, listening to her boys' chatter and take in the green, she could blame them to hell and back. A dash of bitter emerged on her young face, tightening the wrinkles around her eyes into crow's feet.

Raynard reached out and touched the steering wheel, close to the hand that gripped it. He looked up at her and began to speak. William cut him off with a shout of delight.

"Mama! Look!" the eleven-year-old's huge hand shot through the narrow space between Thelma's seat and the window. He cranked her window down and pressed his forehead to the headrest, hovering close to her ear.

"Rainbow," William whispered, voice deeper than her daddy's.

Wet air rolled into the car, filling it with the smell of grass and damp earth. Sure enough, a hundred yards off to the right, a faint rainbow shimmered in the morning mist. It stretched across half a fallow field. Just as Thelma started to slow the car down, the sun rose higher and burned the rainbow into invisibility. The boys sighed quietly. Before Thelma could comfort them with the promise of more rainbows, she saw the smiles on their faces, caught the contentment in that sigh. She shook her head slightly and gave their smile back to them. Her chest tightened as she looked at them—Raynard's deep dimples, William's bright eyes, Jesse's high cheekbones already sprouting stubble—but she smiled.

This trip was her gift to them. The boys had never been out of Mississippi, and sometimes Thelma forgot she ever had, though the boys themselves were proof of her sole excursion out of Mound Bayou.

Everyone in town had heard about the clinics where you could plan your children—not just when or how, but who. Most folks rolled their eyes or shook their heads when they heard; many took to praying. They called it trifling city business sure to bring damnation. And couldn't Black folks think of something better to do with their money? Build a school? Or a community center? Fund a church? Anything had to be better than designing babies.

Thelma had heard it all reshelving the books in the library. One thing about folks in Mound Bayou: they loved to come to the library for their conversations. They didn't have to buy anything to spend a few hours, and with most of the community businesses put out of business by the conglomerates in Sunflower County, free space was a precious thing. And though they probably wouldn't even admit it to themselves, folks didn't like to be outside too much.

Especially after the Riders started stringing up boys in Winstonville. Then Fred Hoss found the Charles girl dangling from a sycamore. She was the first of four that the sheriff declared a suicide. Hate crimes didn't exist anymore 'cause things was so equalized now what with everyone having the right to die in undeclared wars right here on American soil. So no FBI. They were busy investigating racial skirmishes all around the state. Apparently, there were just too many Black folks to kill in Mississippi, and Mound Bayou hardly left a mark on the map.

After all the petitions and marches fell short, after all the activists went on to the next disaster site, after the natives failed night after night to keep their property and families safe and the hired security moved on to more lucrative jobs, the folks in Mound Bayou started to change their minds about the whole clinic thing. They started to think they needed someone who was as invested in the town as they were—someone who would want to keep it safe for future generations, as they did. So while they kept up with short-term tactics, they collected pennies from their purses, tucked away the extra dollar from grocery change, and started discussing biogenetics over card games and dinner rolls.

At first they didn't understand they couldn't just send off for some protectors. Thelma was the first to truly realize that they would be babies. And that someone would have to birth those babies. Would have to potty train them, draw out their bee stings with detergent, give them their first taste of strawberry, and then send them out into the night to face the Klan.

"Mama, I'm hungry," Jesse said from the backseat. He pulled at a thread in his jeans, long legs folded under and around the lip of the seat. Next to him, William, head pressed against the roof, chimed in.

"Yeah, Mama, can we eat soon?" he asked.

She looked at Raynard. "You hungry, too?" she asked.

"Yes, Ma'am," he replied. A sly smile crossed his mouth.

"Mama?" Raynard said.

She brushed thick locks from her chestnut face and glanced at him.

"Can I drive?" he asked.

"No, boy," she waved her right hand and set her eyes back on the road.

"But, Mama, Ches and Oday are already driving, and they're four months younger than us," he said.

Thelma knew that. A lot of the children in Mound Bayou drove—cars, buses, even the few solar tractors left in one piece. She herself had learned to drive at thirteen, just before her Grandmama took to the big mahogany bed and never got back out. Thelma, pressed and greased, had driven her and her father to the funeral in her grandmother's prized Masquerade hybrid, shone just as bright as Thelma for the occasion. She led her father to the gravesite and wiped the tears from his blind eyes. All within the first month of learning how to drive.

"Well, I ain't Oday and Ches's mama, now am I?" she answered. Raynard nodded, kept smiling.

They drove past piles of weathered wood planks pulping in the moisture, the last remnants of abandoned farmhouses. Old machinery rusted into sculptures beside them. Thelma wondered if Mound Bayou would look that discarded in another twenty years. With the fires there wouldn't be anything left, she concluded. Her boys were supposed to prevent that future. Her stomach tightened. No cars passed them on the road.

"We'll eat at the Carter home," she said, shifting in the cloth seat, "should be another twenty-five miles or so."

Raynard and William sat quietly, staring out the windows. Jesse stroked his chin. Her boys didn't fidget, never had, like they'd injected some calm with all those alleles and proteins. Of course, warriors probably wouldn't fidget, she thought. Don't fidget, she corrected herself. She didn't have to guess what the boys would be like anymore; they were right here with her. Still, she sometimes caught herself doing it, an old habit.

On the trip to Georgia, Thelma had exhausted her mind. After she'd spent months learning about phenotypes, behavioral genetics, and biogenetic adaptation; going through net portals and public records scouring for any mention of the Carter Center; and convincing the community council and her father that she could do it and should be the one, there was nothing left to do in the high perch of that rickety transport semi but wonder what it would feel like to carry such a baby inside her and who she would meet when it was done.

She'd already named the baby Billy Ray, after her father. When the doctors told her she'd have triplets, Thelma split the name between them and named the last after the nurse, Jessenia, who held her hand and sang "Duerme de mi Niña" while they peeled Thelma back like an overripe fruit and wrestled the boys out. The doctor guffawed at their size. Thelma wasn't surprised. Her legs hadn't had the strength to lift her after the second trimester.

At eleven, the boys already had to look down at her 5'3" frame. Thelma pulled over to the road's soft shoulder, parked next to a field bordered by tall grass and a dense row of pink and yellow flowers.

"Y'all wanna stretch your legs?" she asked.

The doors were open before she finished the question. She killed the engine and joined the boys. Outside it was cool and moist, the sun losing its fight to dodge the clouds. Thelma didn't mind. She relished having to pull her sweater closer to her shoulders as she hitched one leg up and leaned against the hood. She watched as Jesse walked toward the high grass that sprouted a few feet from the road. William walked farther down, and Raynard up, before they too moved into the brush. Their eyes scanned back and forth, knees bent slightly. Thelma didn't think the boys realized that they walked in formation, that they always had. When the Woods walked through town, Billy and Ray flanked her sides, Jesse bringing up the rear. When she'd realized what they were doing she'd tried to break them from the habit. It lasted all of three days. She couldn't stand to see them cast their eyes everywhere, breathing unevenly, losing the rhythm of their own steps. Right there next to the First Federal she told them to forget what she'd said, and they floated back to their positions, like magnets in easy alignment, she their precious center. She'd never again tried to suppress their instincts.

Even last week when she'd come across William's smoke-stinking clothes soaking in the basin behind the house. She stood there staring down at the gray-pink water, the freckles of blood on the cuff that floated above the surface. For how long she didn't know.

Today William wore the cranberry button-down the girl had brought him. It stretched across his chest as he turned to wave at Thelma, motioned for her to come join them. All clear, she thought, as she lifted her foot from the bumper and walked toward the tall grass.

William had enough sense not to tell Thelma what happened. But the news came quickly enough. Not two hours after she'd found the clothes, Ms. Johnson's granddaughter, Eileen, stood at her door with a plate of fresh rolls and a side of ham from the hog her family had butchered a month ago. No one had brought Thelma anything as precious as ham since she'd finished nursing the boys. She looked at the girl cautiously. In the afternoon light Thelma could see the shadow of a bruise forming under one eye, caught the same sooty smell from the girl's hair, and knew this food was for something William had saved her from. Thelma didn't even want to know that much but held no malice toward the child and so took the food gently and started to thank her for her family's kindness when Old Ms. Johnson interrupted the gratitude with the steady knock of her cane up the wooden steps.

Eileen moved to the side and took her grandmother's elbow as the older woman reached the doorway. In old age Mae Johnson had started to look like a walnut—brown, creased, and round. Only the cane and her aqua floral dresses proved she hadn't completely crossed over into this new incarnation.

"Afternoon, Thelma," she said, smiling.

"Afternoon, Ms. Johnson," Thelma answered. Courtesy said Thelma should invite her in, but she didn't want that story coming in with her so she hesitated. In that second the old woman turned to her granddaughter.

"Eileen, wait for me," she said. Her gaze pointed at the stand of trees next to the front steps.

With a "Yes, ma'am," Thelma and Ms. Johnson stood alone on the porch in the hazy afternoon light. Flecks of ash danced around their faces. One or two settled on Ms. Johnson's plaits, got lost in the white.

"Thelma Ann," Ms. Johnson said, looking up at her, "peace of mind is precious." The weight on the last word made Thelma study Ms. Johnson's face. She squinted at the old woman. Who was she to tell Thelma her duty when Ms. Johnson had no idea what it felt like to be Raynard, Jesse, and William's mother? Brought into this world to restore the community's peace of mind, the specter of her boys' fate had left Thelma awake at night and sleepwalking through the day, always wondering "when"?

Ms. Johnson rapped her cane loudly on the floor.

"Those boys, those Riders, they almost stole Eileen's peace of mind." Ms. Johnson's voice started to tremble, then settled in its depths.

Thelma's eyebrows tensed. She stopped anticipating the words and heard them.

"I told her to leave the salvaging to the men. Merigold ain't no place for her, especially at night. Her and that Thompkins Boy went. Didn't even wait till the fire died out. That Thompkins ran off, left her to 'em. Billy"—she looked over at her sixteen-year-old granddaughter, caught the girl's full eyes for a moment, then swung her head back to Thelma's—"saved her peace of mind."

Out beyond the high grass the boys were being themselves: Jesse tumbling through somersaults and back handsprings, a soft whoosh of air punctuating each exertion; Raynard peering intently at a goldenrod; William sitting in the bough of an oak tree, big feet dangling down.

"Mama," William called down. She looked up through the branches, sweeping a dreadlock from her face.

"Can we eat here?" he asked. He looked back out across the land. "I don't see nothin' for miles."

"Y'all that hungry?" she asked.

"Yeah!" Jesse and Raynard said.

She didn't know if it was safe to eat here right next to the road. They hadn't seen another car once they got off the highway, and state troopers were underfunded right out of existence years ago, but still ...

William spoke up.

"It'll be all right, Mama." He glanced at his brothers, and they nodded in assent.

Her lips pursed. The boys gazed calmly back. "All right then."

Jesse ran past her to the car. The youngest by twelve minutes, Jesse was smaller than his brothers and as they all knew, considerably faster—faster than anyone Thelma had ever known. If the middle school or even Kennedy Memorial were still open, Thelma knew her baby would be a track star. As it was, she enjoyed watching him run almost as much as he seemed to enjoy the chance to unfurl those long, sinewy legs and get gone. She walked over to Raynard and rested her hand against his wide back.

"What you got there?" Thelma asked.

"Solidago virgauria." He brushed his thick finger against the cluster of small yellow flowers. "Don't see many down home."

"Hey, Ray," William called. "What are those?"

He pointed to the dense outcropping of pink and yellow blossoms that covered the land twenty feet beyond the oak tree. From this distance Thelma could see the flowers sprouted at least an acre or two farther into the field. Nothing else grew around them, even grass.

"I don't know," Raynard answered. He began to walk to the flowers.

Jesse returned with the big insulated sack of food and an old blanket.

"Right here, Mama?" he asked.

"No," she answered, "let's eat over there." She pointed at the spot Raynard moved toward. William jumped the fifteen feet from his perch, landed on his feet with a soft thud. Jesse handed him the sack of food and pulled up the rear.

Raynard seemed to have forgotten all about the food. His gaze scanned the river of blossoms, resting for a moment on the stout light green stems, then the large thick leaves growing in bushels. Up close, they could see white blossoms mixed in with the pink and yellow, floating three feet above the ground. Raynard reached out to touch a leaf.

"Careful," Thelma warned, "they're sticky."

He stroked the leaf delicately between his thumb and middle finger. Releasing it, he rubbed his fingers together, felt the gummy residue.

"What are they?" William asked again.

"Live Forevers," Thelma said. She took the blanket and spread it out a few feet from the flowers.

While they ate, Thelma told them more about Live Forevers.

"It's a real old-fashioned plant—old-fashioned even to my Mama. It takes over everything. Grass won't grow around it because it's so thick. It doesn't give in. That's why they've been around for centuries. And—" Thelma put down her ham sandwich and walked over to the nearest leaf. She plucked it from the stem and squeezed its milk out—"you can do this."

As the boys watched, she wiped the tip of the leaf and slowly blew into it. The leaf expanded outward, its veins arching. She pulled it away from her mouth and held it up at its tip, trapping her breath inside. She passed the small, oblong balloon in front of first Raynard, then Jesse's and William's stilled faces.

"Plus," she continued, "you can make a whole new plant with one leaf."

The boys began to chew again but glanced every now and then at the flowers.

Back on the road, Raynard played with the leaf he'd picked before they left. Occasionally, he stole glances at his mother's hands on the steering wheel. In the back Jesse teased William about Eileen, plucking at the shirt the girl brought William two nights before.

"I think she wants to marry you, Billy," Jesse said in a pseudoserious baritone. "Yeah, she's fixin' on being a Woods. Already picking out your clothes."

William examined his brother coolly from across the seat, eyes almost shut from squinting so hard.

"You really need a psych scan, you know that?" William said. He shook his head sadly and looked out the window. Jesse kept up his banter.

Thelma smiled into the rearview mirror at them. It was true the Johnson girl came around a lot, but to Thelma their quiet conversations seemed more companionable than romantic. Jesse was the son she'd have to worry about when it came to girls. Whatever they'd done to the hormones seemed to have a different effect on her youngest. William and Raynard got bigger; Jesse got hornier. She laughed to herself—wicked, but true. This only made his running diatribe funnier. She and Raynard exchanged a knowing glance.

"I'm just saying, Billy. Mrs. William Woods and you ain't even thirteen! That's a waste, man. Total loss."

"And just what is that supposed to mean, Jessup?" Thelma asked. Her relaxed shoulders belied the sharp tone.

William smiled and turned to Jesse.

"Yeah, Jessup. What's that supposed to mean?" he echoed.

Raynard put the leaf in his pocket and turned around in his chair, meaty hands hanging over the headrest. He cocked his head and joined the other two in staring Jesse down.

Under their combined gaze, Jesse smiled weakly, shifted his legs farther across the aisle. Looking up to answer his mother, relief suddenly broke across his face. He pointed through the windshield.

"Is that it up there, Mama?"

Thelma looked where he pointed. Thought to catch her breath, hummed instead.

"Most likely," she answered.

Thelma drove another quarter mile in the silent car. Pulled over into the grass.

Day had fully risen. Evergreen, maple brown, and sky blue radiated from the landscape. In the branches of nearby maple trees, gray squirrels chased each other in tight ellipses. Clouds of gnats swirled like dust in pockets of light. A honeysuckle scent, carried by the breeze, crossed the road, lingered, and then changed direction.

All this was lost on the family sitting in the beat-up Verlanda that had carried them 500 miles from the inevitable to the birthplace of possibility.

The Woods sat silently, collecting their thoughts. They breathed as one. Thelma used her breath to clear her mind, so she could simply sit and witness. William got out first. He touched Jesse's shoulder, then slid out, and waited by his mother's door, scanning the horizon.

As she took her first steps forward, her boys gathered around her.

The sight of what should have been Ezekiel Carter's boyhood home was as familiar to them as the path from Merigold to Mound Bayou. Someone had burned it, burned the house down, scorched the land. The trees even kept their distance. Ten paces lay between them and the hardy shrubs that tried to hide the shame. It had been years. That was obvious. How many, Thelma couldn't tell. Fire had devastated the land around Mound Bayou since the boys were five. This seemed a bit older. Thelma stared at the open space—bare of marker, memorial, or explanation. She stared at it as she had stared at William's sullied clothes: her mind moving swiftly as the truth crept from the torrent of her thoughts. That day she had realized that the boys had done their own laundry for two years. Simply started after a patrol one day. By the time she heard the scrubbing, they already stood shirtless in their summer shorts, hanging each garment carefully on the line outside. She'd looked at them from the back porch, smiling to herself in a plum sunset, thinking she had such sweet boys, such responsible boys.

Realization came quicker the second time around. She turned to Raynard, Jesse, and sweet William, opened up her smile.

"We ought to get back on the road if we wanna get to Ms. Dullah's before supper. That's the softest bed between here and home." She tossed a look back at what they'd come for.

"Y'all ready?" she asked.

William looked at Jesse, Raynard at the edge of the parched earth, then at his brothers.

"Yes, Ma'am," Raynard answered.

Thelma pulled out her keys, swung them in a slow circle around her finger. The sun glinted on the ring, reflected it on her face.

"Ray, you go first. Then William. Then Jesse."

The boys looked at her quizzically.

"There's only thirty miles before we hit the highway. Let's make the most of it." Thelma sauntered toward the passenger side.

Comprehension dawned on Raynard's face, and he grinned fit to split, expertly caught the keys Thelma tossed at him. Jesse opened the door for her with a broad sweep of his hand.

"Madame," Jesse sang.

"Thirty miles, Ray. That means you got ten minutes," William added from the backseat.

Thelma's scoff turned into a laugh.

"Billy, you got a sunstroke or something? Try twenty, maybe even forty minutes if y'all don't take this seriously."

Thelma sat back in her seat and carefully instructed Raynard on how to turn over the ignition. The Verlanda rumbled to life. Looking at Raynard, Thelma thought someone would have to grease their teeth to smile so big. Jesse and William grinned just as wide. As Raynard downshifted around a corner and the gears grinded their dissatisfaction, she worried for a second. But by the time

Jesse rolled to a stop just before the on-ramp, she had to admit the boys took to it quick. Like they'd been born to do it.

Release, in A minor

Clyde played his trumpet cleanly into the hollow. The notes floated across the lake and out into the rising shade of night. They bent around the cypress trees, dipped into the water, and stretched out of Baton Rouge toward the City. He'd received his training there. Muskrat still fresh on his clothes, he left the Delta to show New Orleans what he had. In the end, though, he missed the waters, the slow easy gait of those who didn't have a plane to catch or a roll of film to capture the Garden District, so he came back east, leaving the smoky barrooms and house parties to unravel the lives of other men.

When he first moved to Baton Rouge, this used to be his spot, and in some ways it still was. He didn't need to go downtown, buy anyone a Hurricane, and make small talk. He didn't even have to lean his 6'4" frame into a sparse corner and rub himself absentmindedly, telling the men in the room what lay solid and long beneath his denims. No, Clyde was the sort of beautiful Black man that could open noses just going through his day. His brilliance preceded him into every space and beckoned you to turn around and see what that feeling was, warming you from behind. "Le Appeleurf," they called him. The Summoner. That was in New Orleans. Here they just called him Clyde, and at the refinery, Mr. Tonnerre.

Most days he left work a little early, just as day started to break over the horizon, to come down here and play for his favorite audience the darkened bayou. He could play as purely as he pleased. There was no one to notice the drizzle that began with his blues or the last fat drops staggering out of the sky as the final note faded. The bayou never accused him of conjuring his power. It never begged him to teach it how to play like that or introduce it to the devil who'd given him the gift. It knew who it was and to what it belonged. The bayou had never led a life that left it exposed and aching to be summoned. So it was safe to play here, knowing only he heard.

He let go of lucid thought and let his mind wander. As the notes climbed up the scale, he dove into memory and pushed its power through the horn.

Tony was on all fours, Clyde behind him. He held Tony's hips and reached into the pretty brown catch, stopping only when flesh met flesh and he could go no farther. Here, he dug in a bit more in short rounded thrusts, curling up from the bottom of his tailbone. Sweat misted out of his flesh and slicked down him, pooling at the point of connection. The streaks reflected the moonlight, lit him up as his hands flowed up the swain's back, rubbing the tight muscles to the rhythm of their fucking. Clyde neither knew nor cared if the men sharing the woods could see them. They must have heard the man beneath him, heard the strong moans passing through his lips.

Clyde quickened his stroke, squeezed Tony's thighs, and held his man from beneath. The pulse of him thundered in his ears. Lightning flashed behind his closed lids. He leaned over, pressing himself closer to the strong body pushing itself upon him, and wrapped his arms around Tony's stomach. Lightning lit up the clouds hovering over the lake. Now there was only breath, sharp intakes that rattled his cherry lips and wet the side of Tony's neck. They squeezed tighter until instinct took over and Clyde's hips bucked powerfully, Tony swinging back from the elbow and shoulders, crushing the air between them. Pale blue light forked across the sky. Dirt flew away from the grooves their bodies had dug in the soft earth. They were sounds and movement concentrated on release. Tony's satisfaction arched out of him, wetting the ground between his arms. He kept moving until Clyde followed, throwing his chest out into the night air, his head hinged back, his mouth open. Lightning photographed him—captured the thick chiseled chest, the black dots of nipples, the veins outlined in his forearms. He fell back onto the ground, bringing Tony with him so that they were chest to back once again. The weight of his head made a wet impression on Tony's shoulder. He breathed evenly, blowing cool air onto his lover's back. He felt the body beneath him come to attention, the neck swing slowly from side to side.

"Look," Tony whispered, his chest falling heavily into him. Clyde didn't move.

"Tell me what you see," he replied calmly, playing with the hair on Tony's stomach.

"Clyde—" he began, pointing out in front of him.

"No. Fill your eyes and tell me what you see."

For a second more his back remained tense. He turned to his lover, craning his neck to come eye-to-eye.

"I saw magic." he paused, waiting for reproach. None came. "Balls of fire in the sky ... over there," he says, pointing off to the left, "and there."

Clyde rested his chin on Tony's shoulder and looks up into his eyes, a smile playing at his lips.

"Ball lightning," his voice soft, satiated. "No one knows what causes it."

"You've seen it before?" he asked, wonder calming his tone.

"Every time I cum here," Le Appeleurf replied. "Every time."

~

Lightning flashed against the closed lids. Clyde opened his eyes, letting the memory fade from his mind's eye. He continued his song. Between two sharp notes, he included a riffed love note to that young man long ago lost to the world and mellowed the tone.

He reminded himself to bring the mute next time so he can recount the businessman from Shreveport who offered him his soul to warm his bed. Or maybe he'll practice his finger work and try to boil his mama's funeral out of his veins. His leg vibrated. He removed the phone from his pocket, told his man he'll be home soon, and climbed into the truck, trumpet under his arm, headed out of the back roads.

Wake

Like everything since the epidemic began, I have to jerry-rig what I need. There are no fins or wetsuits on the accessible floors. It's an office building, ill-equipped as anything else for the fall. So I stand at a corner of the roof, overlooking the flood, ripping apart laptop sleeves that I hope will insulate me from the cold winter water a few feet below.

Someone screams. It's far away, so only stops me for a second. It sounds enough like my own to spur me, though. Besides, behind the gloom that covers the city, daylight's burning, and this fix won't last.

I must make the 100 meters or so to the next building—and then there will be the next, and the next. It's the only way left—no more roads. They're under water with everything else. The swim here acquainted me with my new strength's limits. I can fight the current, still move my arms when I can't feel them, and breathe in the smoky air. But even the last of the fever can't keep me warm.

Ice is usually the worst part of Virginia winters, but usual shifts by the hour. Today it's the wind. It whips over the water and stings my wet face. I can't feel it on my extremities.

I look down at my ashy hands. The ghost of a birthday manicure left red chips on the nail tips, but the rest of the color is fading. My skin has cooled to a color more sallow than brown. I won't get much farther if my hands go dead, but I don't see anything in the misty, midday murk to protect them. Nothing but cars and a few bodies float by in the muck below.

The going'll be much worse here, the possibility of injury greater. I've made it well into downtown but still can't see my destination. Smoke obscures the James Monroe Building and everything else beyond the next block.

Soon enough I'll drown in guilt—I can't expect and don't deserve any better but first, I'll scale the Monroe and leave Grayl's careworn piece of paper on its precipice. After that I don't give a damn about the end's particulars.

I know there'll be screaming and that goddamn cloud, isn't much else left to know.

I tie telephone cord around the neoprene swatches on my legs, tighten the knot holding my dreadlocks back, and ease myself down into the flood.

I watch my toes, ankles, legs disappear into the murk.

As my shoulders break the surface, fat drops of rain begin to fall. Of course. Cursing, I start my stroke, carefully pulling what's left of the world into my wake.

As ever, the cloud menaces from above.

It rolled into Richmond in mid-October, a stubborn mist that hung low on the horizon.

The cloud didn't travel, wouldn't dissipate—just incrementally grew gargantuan as it ate up the autumn sky. By Halloween the full moon looked like a bright dot against it.

The next day came the rain.

Though it only fell from that cloud, right away things started to disintegrate: Fights filled the streets; intermittent screaming was everywhere and then always; premeditated pile-ups began to block 64 and Powhite; a great-grandmother in Montrose set her entire neighborhood ablaze one quiet Sunday morning; over the span of a few hours, five different semis crashed into Colonial Market Mall to chase down the people inside, then the first responders, and finally the crew tasked with demolishing the ruins ...

I lost track of the atrocities.

I do know that all that time, the rain slowed to a drizzle, but never quite stopped.

The water tastes awful. When I turn my head between strokes to breathe, thin streams invade my mouth. Putrefaction, it turns out, has a flavor. It is as horrible as it is inescapable. It rivals the yells that I can't track or elude as they bounce around the buildings.

Nauseated, saliva pools under my tongue; I turn my head to spit. And thirty feet away a group of bloated bodies bobs. They've collected in a bank vestibule, pushed there by the current and held by the unexpected opening. A memory surfaces: an undergrad professor who pontificated for two hours on the merits of vestibules and their surprising intimacies. It almost makes me laugh, but I stop myself. I can't let my mind drift away. Drifting leads to floating. I swim.

The flood sloshes in my ears. Thankfully, it muffles the screams. But even if I keep my eyes closed and only snatch glances ahead to keep myself moving straight, there's no avoiding the sickening tang of chemicals and rot.

At first the mayhem seemed like one of those seasons of violence—weird, but not altogether strange, something like that rain.

Then came Thanksgiving. Folks from Short Pump to Midlothian picked up the nearest carving knife and slashed their way through the generations. It unmoored the city.

We drifted into a brutal territory, where going to work or waiting for the bus became an accidental act of bravery.

In the old Richmond, I knew porticoes, friezes, and the perfect parabola to hold tons of steel and concrete suspended in mid-air. I was the reformed poet turned respected architect, a chosen daughter though I had no family left.

But there were gaps in my education. I didn't even know what I didn't know.

I hadn't known, for instance, that horror could actually take your breath away.

Then the last day I went to the office, I saw a young family—mama with babe in arms—pile into a car and cruise down Grace Street, lobbing Molotov cocktails at other cars, passersby, and the bus enclosure below my office window. As flames erupted, the family screeched—their mouths twisted and awful, every tooth visible. Both parents and the red-faced infant rose to the same shrill decibel. The sound pierced the glass at the corner of my office where I stood transfixed.

And in what should have been the next breath, my lungs stopped. I didn't forget to breathe. Until they passed and rounded the corner, I simply couldn't.

I've learned a lot since that morning, very little of it welcome knowledge.

Take this: a few days before the New Year, the government issued tickets for evacuation buses that never showed up. That long day and night, as folks realized they never would, I sat in City Stadium's main parking lot, the useless ticket balled in my fist and a moist rag tied over my mouth. I watched the shadows of people, backlit by fire, shuffle back out into wet hell. As they went, I saw their last bits of hope pop! like blown bulbs. It was my first time seeing people extinguished.

It made me lie down on the asphalt and hold my churning stomach. The echo of the red-faced child rang in my head. I tried to ignore it, counted backwards from ten. When I could open my eyes without gagging I watched fire planes roar overhead as they dumped retardant in bright orange trails that lit up the sky.

~

Even with the neoprene, the cold seeps in. Each kick of my legs sends pinpricks down my hips to toes that no longer itch with cold, but the more I move the less I feel it.

Something soft slides past me underwater. I push it away, quicken my stroke. A box bay window, separated from its house, floats into my path, knocked by something under the surface. There's no time to dodge it.

It digs in, down the length of me. Sharp pain scratches down my side, finding the flesh between the coverings, and I lose my rhythm.

At the New Year, when the rain subsided to mist, the James River overflowed its banks and the lower half of Richmond flooded. I realized then that the liquefying of the city could not be stopped. I counted my food store for the umpteenth time and lay in bed for days. The very same afternoon the delirium passed and I could stand, the rain returned in earnest—never enough to put out the fires, only add the sound of sizzle to the screams.

Most of the city had batshat weeks before, so no one much noticed. Those who did moved to higher ground.

I met Grayl there, at the top of a hill turned makeshift island.

Thinking her name weighs me down. But there, under neoprene sleeves, the light scratch of the plastic bag tucked into my bra spurs me, and I pull harder, stay afloat.

The frigid water begins to dull the pain from the laceration. I crawl forward, regain my rhythm in four painful strokes. Finally, the next building is within reach.

I grab onto the corner of it and drag myself slowly around the perimeter, onto its north side and the next block. From there I can see two men on a rooftop a few doors down. Their arms are akimbo. I can't tell if they're signaling to me or in a frenzy.

I swim the opposite direction, careful to keep my head underwater, my ears covered.

That precious, dry piece of property on top of the hill held ten people—Grayl, Rita, Jen, DaQuan, Joshua, Charles, Theresa, Bill, and Santi. Thousands of others surrounded us. Legions of used-to-be grandpas, recently lovers, and not-quite children screeched through the submerging streets. Their path of destruction encircled us.

We couldn't help but listen to them havoc one another and the few uninfected who survived, for a time, amongst them. We ten slept in shifts, our backs to each other in a tight circle, each one sticking to the other, tacky with the dirt and sweat of months wearing the business casual clothes and uniforms that suited our old lives, but not sufficiently the fall of Virginia.

When I could sleep I had the same dream: sinking, an endless descent in a broken boat. The boat took on water no matter what I tried or where I searched the hull for defects. I always woke exhausted, jolted back to reality by the madness just beyond our shrinking shore.

On our makeshift island we fared better, but it took ingenuity.

We papered over the holes in our hearts with reclaimed tickets.

I don't know who first wrote their wishes on an evacuation ticket, but I was sitting near the edge of the island when the first one floated up and stuck.

I showed it to Grayl, who brought it to the others. When more tickets showed up the next day, Grayl took it as a sign. She said that we could honor the ticket holder by fulfilling the wishes scribbled on each one.

Horseshit, of course, but purposeful.

Collecting the tickets provided an activity besides foraging for and rationing food; trying to decipher them brought us together for more than protection. But mostly I did it because I thought it would keep us from killing each other for a while.

I flip onto my back. It's dangerous not to see what's coming toward me or up from below, but I have to conserve energy. I backstroke tentatively to avoid debris and try not to think of how I resemble the floating corpses. Above me, the sky roils, a sickly pink that would've meant a tornado before. It's hard to tell what things mean now.

Save the cloud and color, the air is empty. The fire planes disappeared about the time the last of the electricity flickered off. I assume the fire had eaten through the remaining viable lines. And that the planes moved somewhere that could still be saved.

There have been no news leaflets dropped or announcements over the loud speakers for three weeks. Cell towers went out first. Everywhere else remains a mystery.

The tickets worked.

I didn't murder Grayl and the others for eighteen days. I'd started thinking we must be immune, but today I woke up, apparently sometime after the drowning dream and found the ruin of them. My hands were tacky with blood.

I hollered till I hollowed.

I didn't know that anyone woke from the sickness. I hadn't fathomed that the people screaming might just as easily have been like I am now—dead on the inside, crushed by what they'd done, but alive.

I didn't know that anguish could sound exactly like mindless rage or that sometimes broken fevers kept breaking until they shattered what remained.

~

We all wrote our unspent wishes. "Just as a precaution," Grayl had said. I like that about her: her kindness, even here. Even now. Evidently she was scared of heights. It must have taken all of her will to keep climbing when everything in her wanted to stay close to the ground. "Go to the top of the tallest building in the city," her ticket read.

After I woke, I couldn't find any of the others' tickets or my own, but Grayl held hers close to her heart in a little plastic bag that now scratches me with every stroke.

Just a few more miles to go.

I don't know where the strength comes from—if it's the last of the sickness coursing through me or something that lay dormant or cloaked all along, but I will not quit. It doesn't matter how long it takes. I will stand on the 29th floor of the James Monroe and see what's left beneath.

The Hell You Say

You know country people. They do country shit to you. Like hang you headfirst from a hotel balcony, or threaten you with their grandaddy's gun like she did me, or curse you quiet so you don't know calamity's running your way, intent on dragging your ass.

You know, country shit.

What?

You got to admit, things get thick and tricky here from a look or a missed pardon. Back in Chi, ain't that way. Well ... it's different. Trust me.

Look, man, I was trying to help her. She can't do what I do: stand in front of shopkeepers, production heads, and publishers pitching her wares from west coast to east. That costs, and with my success rate it don't come cheap. Maybe out here two bits and a handshake will get you something, but nothing you want to keep.

Look, that is what it was about. Still, percentages aren't worth a fight—much less sitting in this cell, waiting to shuffle and yessuh my way back to freedom.

Shit yes, I will. We may both be colored, but this is her territory.

My mentor could plant a seed in a person's mind that would root quick and choke out what did not support it, feed what did. It was more than a gift. It was a power. Some say power is a dangerous thing for a woman to have.

I say it's the only way to live. You just have to wield it well.

Take that trouble today. You think the sheriff would've listened to me if I hadn't? With that fella oppugning my character, even whilst you pried his fingers off a tire iron? No, sir.

So that's how I spend my time, not worrying about what ignorant folks say.

As a business woman, I focus on what they read. Claudette called herself a conjurer, but I prefer more flexible terms.

When your time comes and your way's clear, you'll decide your title.

Just remember that most folks only know what you make it easy to. That's why everyone in town knows my signs, but not what they do. You're right, soon the handmade papers and printing press, too.

He isn't the only paper salesman in the world. You found him; you can find another.

Look, Esquire, use those fancy credentials to get me outta here.

Again with the contracts? Shit, if I'd signed the first one you gave me I'd be in business with that crazy heifer and then where would I be?

This ain't the time for jokes. Fine. Maybe I wouldn't be in jail. No. You know *what*? Maybe I would.

I ain't signing nothing, man.

Do you know why Claudette spoke spells when she had all that power sitting in the back acres? Control.

A whisper wish you put out in the world with words. There are bones and baubles to back it, but the speaking makes it manifest. How it's spoken lets you lead the thing and dictate its force.

You can't do that with the water in that back well. It's too potent. We cut it to keep it safe. Claudette tried farming with it, but that's the summer lightning bugs spelled-out commands in the fields—took two weeks of gris gris to convince folks otherwise.

After that harvest (and days, I mean days, of grinding and storing wheat), she taught herself to blacksmith. She nearly cursed up a storm in the process, and the smoke turned her blonde hair brown—but she mastered it. Spent early mornings and sweltering nights hammering and bending tools into being. Then I'd fetch a trough of well water to cool what she made. Even the steam sparkled with possibilities. Us both sitting there, breathing it in, full of cornucopia bread and new power churning through us, she said to me, "Viv, I believe I've found my way. Where you going?"

I thought about it 'til I couldn't keep another thought in my head. I wanted my work to last, and looking over the discarded notes from Claudette's mentor, I found my way.

To last, my business need not be born in the world, only in folks' minds. Claudette didn't know 'cause she couldn't do it: reading plants the seed the deepest.

Now, much as I love books I can't write worth a lick, so I took up a chisel still warm from the fire and crafted my first sign, a rough old "Welcome" that still hangs on the front porch. Not my best work, but a good start. It brought you through the front door. Don't worry. It's the last work I put in you, except for these biscuits of course. You want another?

I use a tray she made to mold the handmade paper. Her cylinders are the heart of the printing press. You'd be surprised all the places Claudette's magic fits.

No one could craft a useful, lovely lie quite like Claudette, but by the time she passed she'd mastered the foundry and the anvil, too. Your contracts are the next step on that path.

Too few people believe in magic. That's why there's so little of it in the world. So the more mundane we make it, the better.

So you gonna help me or not?

Man, stop pushing that contract at me!

I knew I shouldn't have come out here! I can't stand these hick towns, always a nightmare—hot, backwards, full of simple Negroes and crazy-ass White people. But hey, here they even managed to get that backward.

I can't imagine why you came back here.

I told Sonny this backwater would be hell! I told him. Only thing worse than coming is staying.

Shame about him, but the mind is only soil—fertile or fallow dictates how true the thing grows.

You'd do well to remember that.

I'm not accusing, not at all. I know you were playing meek, but you got to read people. Meek doesn't always work. You can't let folks bully you. Vincent should have signed the contract before you set a meeting with me. Sure, I could have put something on him, but something in them must make it true. Otherwise it won't last. Look at Jim Crow.

I never thought I'd see it teetering. When Claudette predicted it, I told her she mistook other White folks for herself, but she saw true—decades early, and that wasn't even her gift.

Now I don't know about most, but enough folks want to do better. We grease the way.

No, I'm not saying good is inevitable. It ain't. Or that folks can't do it on their own. They can. A person just gets tired waiting on someday where there's a perfectly good Tuesday coming right up.

It's good to see you smile. I know you're vexed, but

there's only so much we can do; he drank it straight. Not much to temper that—maybe if we pool our power, layer the thing, but that's still a maybe.

Speaking of which—car trouble or not, you mustn't bring anyone to the land. If we'd met at the office like we planned, he would have passed plenty a' handiwork on the way. The do-no-harm in the apothecary sign alone would have settled him.

If your apprenticeship succeeds, you'll become the steward of this land ... one day. Until then, I decide who visits. The no-trespassing signs are plenty when you don't shield folks. Understand?

Good. I know. That comes with being an apprentice. And most won't be like him, not to you, anyway. It's part of the reason I chose you. I know you think it's 'cause of your schooling and the places you can go because of what's between your legs, but you have a talent for arbitration. I'm interested to see how it shapes your abilities.

Just don't take it too far. Know your limits—or make some.

You see I looked the other way when he pissed on Claudette's gladiolas and broke branches for sport. But once he helped himself to the well?

That's another thing.

I just got some water. Look, I'm sweating like a hog, walking all that way in my suit, mind you to try and do business, and she gonna pull a rifle on me!

Ain't folks supposed to be hospitable down here?!

Shit yeah, I raised that tire iron. I told her the same as I'm telling you—"Beg some wench's approval? I'll be damned."

~

What kind of natural born fool says something like that down a wishing well?

She provoked me. I had to protect myself.

I know what is, what isn't, and most assuredly, what ain't. He chose.

I told him it was the family wishing well. That doesn't take belief. Respect should have stopped him from taking a second sip.

He called his trouble.

Are you trying to say this is my fault? The hell you say!

What do you mean "exactly"?

Hey, man! Where you going?

Up Jumped the Devil

The Devil ran 24 hours a day, in hot weather and cold, free days and curfewed, shuttling folks from the catacombs to the Quarters three stories above. It did not stop for maintenance, bad weather, or bodies on the track. Policy dictated that the schedule must be kept, so to hell with each and every other thing. The women and men riding knew policy as well as they knew the number of hours required for a week's rations and safe passage back to the limestone tomb where their families waited for them down below.

As Mure rode shoulder to shoulder with the workers for the first time, she did not question this unceasing dedication, or why they moved as fluidly and constantly as the workings of a clock, even if it only brought them that much closer to the end of their days. Nor did she feel her father's foolish pride in upholding the world that stood on top of them, each reinforced steel story of it reaching heights that they would never know. She sat amongst the workers now because he no longer could, and she wouldn't tell him that she'd rather him perish than trade precious moments of her gray and dirty life.

She and her father had not been born to the Combs, but were brought there, allowed to escape the carcinogenic winds and scalding precipitation that plagued the city after the drop. That first rainy, scorching night they came to the Combs, Mure wandered away from their group, trying to escape the pain inside her head. Instead, she found an immense door in the face of a mountain. She alerted their small group, and together they watched the door open, meager weapons at the ready, dreading what might come. Mure stood between her father and Ailey, who only spoke three words but fought fiercely whenever necessary. She felt safe between them.

When men draped in nylon parkas emerged and offered them refuge, members of their group laughed with relief, Ailey loudest of all. After the men explained it would be in exchange for servitude, the laughter ceased. Still, Ailey whispered "should" even as the smile fell from his face.

Sanctuary cost one worker from each household. With their last meal a fading memory, the group agreed. Her father did not ask if she would earn their keep, though she'd been grown a long time and his legs pained him just as much as her head hurt her. He touched her cheek with two fingers as he always had, left her with warm, clean food in her hands, and took his place in the workers line. He returned some twelve hours later, tired but attentive as she showed him their new catacomb home. Now ten years had passed and, migraines or not, she would return his kindness.

On this, her first day on the Devil, she kept her gaze forward. People packed the car she sat in and the next two or three in front of it. On her car everyone wore a mechanic's navy coveralls. In the next they donned red, and green in the one in front of that. Far ahead in the farthest car she could see, she spied a woman with long gray hair tied by a purple scarf that matched her coveralls. Mure only knew what a couple of the colors meant. At least the workers were grouped by the color of their clothes instead of their skin. In that, the Combs differed from the hardscrabble world outside. She took a second to savor not enduring her brownness, sat tall in her father's navy uniform, and tried not to think too much of what might wait for her at the end of the line.

Mure would bet she'd seen worse. Thirty-two years on the outside, twelve of them after the drop, almost guaranteed it. Almost. Yet, their descent into the Combs had fostered a glimmer of hope she protected. If that meant this, then so be it. The other workers on her car were quiet, whether because of the early hour or the looming day's work, Mure did not know.

Her father had never told her anything about the Quarters. But last night he dimmed the oil lamp, pulled a chair close to her pallet, and in whispered tones relayed the intricacies of their survival.

As he spoke, his short afro bloomed out into a corona behind him, made majestic by the pale amber crystal that hung above the flame's glow.

"Choose an interior seat and keep your eyes on the car while you ride," he said.

Mure wondered at this but did not speak.

"When you get there it will be dim. There'll be bells to signal, but you can just follow the people ahead of you," he said. Dark she knew; this did not faze her.

"They'll lead you to the anteroom. Take these." He handed her the pair of tinted spectacles she'd seen resting on the mantle each evening they'd had one. "When you hear the first chime, stand, join the line of others and wait. The Devil will take you right to the passage, so just follow the people in front of you when the doors open. You'll need these once you're inside the anteroom."

"Inside, there'll be a smell—thick and sweet. Don't let it bother you. It may hit you hard, clog your sinuses, but it's normal there. They may even spray you with it. It's how they know where we are without looking."

She'd heard rumors that the ones above couldn't see clearly. Soon enough she would know for herself.

"I don't know exactly what you'll be doing. You have the skills, but your work may be different than mine. They try to match you to what they think of you—not who you are. Remember that, Mure."

Dictating identities had caused trouble before. As part of their indoctrination, the men told their group how this place came to be. The ones above had arrived first. No one had to say they were rich; no one else could have afforded to buy a place in the Quarters. A long-dead company built the entire structure on top of the catacombs, hoping to escape the world's undoing. The dwellers above bought into the Quarters before its completion. It boasted the best amenities above and strongest below. Yet, all their measures failed—although no earthquake came, no hurricane that they could not withstand, no marauding hordes. After the drop the very air betrayed all their well-financed designs. When the atmosphere soured, the dwellers stayed inside with their air purifiers and oxygen scrubbers and so had never tested their mettle. Now they were too afraid to see if their lungs could withstand it, if the neurological and physical impairments that fell most of the outside world would bring them low, too. And even if the Quarters remained the only building still standing on once-tony, bustling Icon Avenue, to the dwellers its unique survival degraded their luxury. As there was no longer a basis for comparison, they could only say that they survived relatively unscathed.

This turned out to be the greatest luxury, but to them, insufficient. The ones above devised a plan to procure more support staff to do the things they could not but also some of what they could. They convinced the original concierge to open the underground lock and recruit those outside who could still stand and showed no signs of contagion or psychosis. The recruiters hadn't told her all of this, but in time other people filled in the gaps. The Combs, like every other place, had its secret knowledge, its versions of history.

There'd been an uprising just before their group arrived. Mure knew because a dated plaque, the only shining thing in the tunnels, stood at the Devil's entrance naming those who had "betrayed" the Quarters. It listed the "deserter" names in bas relief so that each one cast a shadow and only the Quarter's name glistened. The plaque made Mure wonder what other riches might lie above.

She heard rumors that after the revolt failed some of the revolutionaries retreated lower, past the reinforced levels into the bowels of the Combs, a network of limestone caves. The rumors said that those people had learned to live completely without the light.

Initially, Mure didn't believe it. Who would leave this sanctuary? No one had in the years she'd spent here. But on those nights when the Combs were especially cold and particularly still, it was hard not to think the scrapings and vibrations at their feet were not the work of something buried even deeper than they were.

She began to wonder what they did all day, the ones below. How did they live? Did they couple and marry? What did they eat? For a while the questions entertained her, but in time only one mattered: could it be?

Four months ago, she confirmed it. As her father's health declined, she sought any means to supplement the food and water provisions that had been cut with his work hours. So she found herself divining for water, tracking a subterranean stream that held the promise of potability and possibly cavefish. There on a black bank, at the edge of a vast darkness, she felt the brush of a hand and a second later hushed breath at her elbow.

Instinct prodded Mure, and she ran, jumping over stalagmites and phantoms. Whoever had touched her did not follow, had not spoken, but would not leave her thoughts.

After that, early each morning, or what they called morning, Mure searched for signs. These meandering walks took her far from the bellows and bangs of life underground. It became the ritual that sustained her. In the dark she discovered precious quiet that eased her headaches. Sitting in the cool tranquility, Mure would still herself and pretend she'd turned to the stone that surrounded her. Even when she sensed a heartbeat, she did not move. She told herself the sensation was fear and nothing more. Once, she woke and found a crystal near her palm. Back at home, she hung it on her lantern. The next morning she struck out as always.

In the depths she let her pain float away. Her fear followed. Surrounded by something or someone she could not see, she no longer dreaded what she might feel next.

Mure cultivated calm there and carried it with her, even now.

The Devil had no conductor. It ran on its own relentless steam, though the folks in the Combs didn't know the exact source of its energy. So Mure could only wait. It would move in its own time. A third bell chimed and slowly it began to chug forward.

She spotted a plastic purple carnation wedged between two tunnel posts. It was for Ailey. She too missed him: both his comforting presence and easy laugh in the face of their fates. Mure had never known anyone better. She would doubt anyone else had either.

His had been one of the bodies left on the track.

He and his mother, Filomena, took on the job of sand painters when they arrived. Filomena had thought she could keep track of Ailey and that the assignment might ease the strain of living within boundaries. Every group had its vocation, and the purple ones, the sand painters, braved the scaffolding that encircled the Quarters to give the dwellers above some of what they had lost: the scenes of somewhere else, places they would never go, in the form of dirt that been carved into.

After years left in the smog, a thick layer of muck covered the Quarters' windows. The sand painters etched into it. Apparently, mother and son excelled at the form because their work hours lengthened and after a time Mure rarely saw them.

Two months ago, Ailey's harness snapped, and he crashed into the wall above the Devil's outside track, tumbling into the tunnel just as it opened to admit the first car.

And lay there. No one would come to collect him or allow his mother to. They maintained the Devil's schedule.

After, some people took to wearing splashes of purple and speaking fondly of Ailey and the frescoes he painted on the tunnels' curved walls. But that was all.

Mure braced herself against the seat. The Devil flew now, barreling toward their destination. As they rode, one of Ailey's stories played out on the tunnel walls. At first she couldn't make out the meaning of the bright green and yellow cylinder, but then a snake's head appeared at the end of it and gobbled up an apple near a curve. It reappeared from a hole and looked perched to strike its next victim.

They rounded a corner and slowed. As if on cue, people on the left side of the car looked down or to the other side—anywhere but where they'd just been gazing. Mure peered deeper into the tunnel and caught a flash of offal.

The others must have learned to look away from what Ailey was left behind. A decomposed hand and shard of bone poked straight up from the ground near the tracks. Just below it, Mure saw something shredded and opalescent, something so covered in insects that it moved.

She squeezed her eyes shut.

The Devil slowed, stopped in a dim corridor. Workers began to rise from their seats. She could see nothing but the gore etched into the inside of her eyelids. When the doors opened on a chime, people moved toward them. Mure followed. As the threshold cleared, she took a step toward the platform.

Pain pierced the top of her head and tried to escape through her eyes. Mure lost her footing. She saw her left hand fly up awkwardly in the air and felt a stab of pain in her left ankle. Collapsing under her weight, the world twirled as she fell. When it stopped, she found herself wedged between the platform and the Devil's formidable flank. Nearly all the cars had emptied. She could see the workers through the windows and on the platform, most with their eyes facing forward. Only one person looked directly at her: a woman in purple with a matching scarf halfway down the platform. Dirt and grime covered the woman's face, obscured it so that it seemed a mask. A single tear rolled down her cheek as she tore her gaze away.

"Help!" Mure yelled. "Help, please!"

A few more heads turned in her direction. No one moved to her.

An older, bearded man lingered at the anteroom's door. A force seemed to pull his gaze back toward her. Mure joined her will to it.

"Please," she said softly. He closed his eyes and slowly swung his head back to center and then down into his chest. He stepped through the anteroom door and away. Others followed.

Mure's breath caught. Real panic began to take over, and just behind it a peace she didn't want to acknowledge. The second bell chimed. Mure began to hyperventilate. Each breath stabbed into her ribs. She looked back at the woman. Perhaps it was a death mask she wore.

Here? Now? This is how she would die? Ripped in two when the Devil next departed?

Mure jerked her gaze around, tried to form a thought.

Like a trick of the light, she saw them emerge. From the tunnel's shadows beyond the third rail of the track, the deserters' tattered parkas dragged the ground as they climbed onto the platform and dispersed silently across the length of the car. Some pushed with their palms from where they stood, and others turned and bowed their backs to get a grip on the Devil's bottom edge.

Two men, tall as trees from where she lay, stood on either side of her, backs flat against metal. They crouched and braced their legs against the edge of the platform. They strained against the enormous weight and ever so slightly the Devil began to tilt. A space between Mure and the metal cracked open. The man on her left called out, and the others dug in, grunting with exertion. The crack widened, and Mure struggled to free herself.

She felt a pair of hands slide under her shoulders and grab her under the armpits. The woman's purple scarf fell down in Mure's face as she tried to move her, tugging with all her might. Mure locked her hands onto the woman's shoulders, and she pushed with her free leg. On the next pull she came free.

The third chime sounded, and the Devil began to move. All but the two deserters above her backed away and headed in the opposite direction. When it moved far enough they jumped down and hurried back into the shadows that filled the wider section of the tunnel. The two closest to Mure crouched just above her. She rolled farther from the edge and looked around. The door to the anteroom stood ajar. The woman with the purple scarf could make it inside if she hurried. For a second she stood suspended.

With a hot gust the Devil plunged back into the abyss.

One of the men reached down to Mure and helped her right herself. She stood, careful to keep her weight on her right ankle. He looked at her warmly.

"You soothe the children," he said. A glinting crystal that hung around his neck caught the light and Mure's attention.

"The littlest ones are still afraid of the dark," he explained.

He nodded into the shadows, a question in his eyes. Mure thought of her father.

She didn't see where the woman with the purple scarf went, but later the tunnels echoed with whispers of a muralless morning, of three words scrawled on every window of the first three floors: "Must." "Ought." "Should."

With those words, Mure recognized Filomena long after they parted.

Mure next saw her near the wreckage caused when the Devil lost its way, left its moorings, and crashed into the tunnel wall. The two women stood side by side, a few steps away from the mechanics piecing together their future.

It could have been broken track, too much speed, or built-up debris. They'd never really know, but they all knew what they knew.

Mure did not question her or offer old condolences. She unfurled the purple scarf from her head and wiped grime from Filomena's face. For the Devil might die, and it was only right to be clean when you got your soul back.

About the Author

Tenea D. Johnson was born in Kentucky. From it, she took the calm of the Ohio River and the swell of honesty (sometimes refreshing, sometimes catastrophic) that afflicts the folks born along its banks. Writing sustains her; music saves her. As often as possible, she straddles their borders. Her musical stories were heard at venues including The Public Theater and The Knitting Factory.

Her short fiction appears in *Mothership: Tales from Afrofuturism and Beyond, Sycorax's Daughters*, and *Blue and Gray: Ghost Stories from the Civil War,* among other anthologies. Her debut novel, *Smoketown*, won the Parallax Award. R/evolution, the first book in the Revolution series (which includes the novel, *Evolution*), also received an honorable mention that year.

Starting Fiction came first, later *Blueprints for Better Worlds*. No doubt she's somewhere tinkering with an arts and empowerment enterprise or perhaps sitting in the sunshine. Her virtual home is teneadjohnson.com. Stop by anytime.